A Bargain

TO DIE FOR

Judy Woodward Bates,

a.k.a. The Bargainomics Lady

BARGAINOMICS PUBLICATIONS

A Bargain to Die For
By Judy Woodward Bates
First Edition, ©2020 by Judy Woodward Bates
All Rights Reserved

ISBN-13: 9780976616627
Also available in eBook

Bargainomics Publications
Cover Art: Judy Woodward Bates, Tim Vines
Cover Concept: Judy Woodward Bates
Cover Graphic Design: Hyliian Graphics
Interior Design: The Author's Mentor, theauthorsmentor.com
Author Photos: Larry W. Bates

The following is a work of fiction. Names, characters, places, and incidents are fictitious or used fictitiously. Any resemblance to real persons, living or dead, to factual events, or to businesses is coincidental and unintentional except where noted in the Acknowledgments and "What's Real?"

PUBLISHED IN THE UNITED STATES OF AMERICA

Dedication

To my Lord and Savior Jesus Christ.

"Great is thy faithfulness"

(Lamentations 3:23b).

ALSO BY JUDY WOODWARD BATES

The Gospel Truth about Money Management

Blessedly Budgeted Women's Events

Bargainomics: Money Management by the Book

ACKNOWLEDGMENTS

I could never name all the folks who've encouraged and inspired me to get this whodunit written. First and foremost, I thank my Lord and Savior Jesus Christ for blessing me with the joy of writing. Next, I thank my handsome and wonderful husband Larry for being my Barnabas and putting up with my absences in both mind and body as I've worked on this book.

Thanks, too, to my reader and critic Shirley Ferguson for all her input. And this book would never have happened without the selfless hours of proofreading by my dear friend, writing retreat pal, and fellow writer Sammie Jo Barstow. Her expertise and encouragement have been invaluable.

I am so grateful to the folks at WBRC Fox 6 TV in Birmingham, Alabama who put up with me and my guest spot for many years, and to my lifelong friend and real-life cousin Millie Caffee, a wonderful artist and my partner in crime and shopping in both real life and fiction.

Finally, to Per Nordstrand, an honest-to-goodness Norwegian police officer who, along with his wife Iren and their children, grandchildren, and extended family are considered family by me and Larry.

While many of the people and landmarks in this work of fiction are real, I've fictionalized the TV station as WEEE to allow myself some leeway for future adventures. Also included are an abundance of fictional people and places. For example, Dupree's doesn't exist, though I sorely wish it did. Art in the Park also comes from my imagination, but my Norwegian friends are all real. My dad, Ellis Woodward, has been in heaven for quite a few years now, but I brought him back – at least, on paper – so he could share in my adventures.

A Bargainomics Lady Mystery

A Bargain
TO DIE FOR

1

Wednesday, 11:32 p.m. "You no-good, low-down piece of garbage moron!" Jewel punctuated her tirade with a highly creative string of profanity and yet another dinner plate, both flung directly at her cowering husband, Ray John Fitzhugh. The bony scarecrow of a man managed to deflect the plate, and it smacked the wall beside him, sending a shower of shards in all directions.

"Now, sugar pie, if you'll just let me explain," Ray John wheedled, both hands shielding his face as he prepared for another onslaught. One eye on Jewel and one on the only exit door of the dilapidated travel trailer the couple called home, he took a stealthy, barefoot sidestep over the remains of their dishes.

"Explain, my eyeball!" Jewel continued at full volume. "What's to explain? You're an idiot! You've got less sense than God gave a goose! How could you be so stupid? If you don't fix this mess, so help me, Ray John, I'm gonna kill you if it's the last thing I do!"

"But honey bear, I just needed somewhere to stash it for a little while. How was I to know that fella was comin' to pick up the box?"

Thursday, 5:02 a.m. Ray John awoke from a fitful sleep, his skinny frame slumped into one of the two decrepit recliners that made up the seating area of the trailer's living room. Silver duct tape worn dull gray covered splits in the chair arms and back while the deflated seat cushion cupped around Ray John's scrawny rear as he sank into its recesses. Phone in one hand and the other rubbing nervously through his tangle of greasy black hair, he swallowed hard for the umpteenth time, then punched in the number.

Ray John's call was received with an unpleasant, "I assume this is urgent." Not only had he awakened The Collector at this absurdly early hour, but he had to tell him what was causing the delay in their transaction. The response was not as dreadful as Ray John had feared.

"So," The Collector's gruff voice breathed into the telephone, "get it back. Simple. Right, Mr. Fitzhugh?" The Collector was the only person who ever addressed Ray John in this manner. "Simple is something I believe you clearly understand."

"Uh, yeah. Sure," Ray John stammered. "So me and you are okay, right?"

"As long as you bring me what I'm paying you for, Mr. Fitzhugh. By whatever means necessary. And in return, as per our agreement, you shall be handsomely rewarded."

2

6:45 a.m. The phone rang. Sleeping mask in place, I stretched an arm toward the irritating chirping and dragged the receiver to my ear.

"Hello?" I croaked. No, I wasn't sick. That's my usual voice when I'm awakened from a fog-deep sleep.

"What time are you picking me up?" asked the all-too-cheery voice of my cousin Millie, who is also my dear friend, my shopping buddy, and my Vanna White (which I'll explain later), not to mention a super-talented painter and sculptor, plus the best grandmother on the planet.

"What time is it?" I muttered.

"6:45."

"What!" This time I shrieked and croaked simultaneously. Shoving my mask onto my forehead, I checked my bedside alarm clock/sound machine (which hadn't made so much as a peep), threw back the covers, and slid my feet over the side of the bed.

4

At my age – 50-something – there's no leaping out of bed except in the event of a house fire or the approach of a crazed killer.

Hobbling straight for the bathroom, phone in hand, I punched the speaker button and parked Millie on the countertop while I proceeded as quietly as possible to relieve my bursting bladder. "I forgot to set the alarm. I hadn't even gotten out of bed when you called," I groaned above the tinkling noises. "I'll have to swing by on my way back."

Ending the call, I managed the fastest shower, makeup, and dressing in history. I bolted out the door, clothed and – more or less – in my right mind. En route through the house, I snagged a caffeine-free Diet Dr. Pepper, the breakfast of decaf champions, out of the fridge.

7:35. In the car and on the road. With the clock in my head ticking like Big Ben, I flipped on my turn indicator and hoped for "the kindness of strangers." Sure enough, a pickup truck hauling huge sheets of plate glass flashed its lights and slowed to let me move over a lane.

7:36. I waved one hand in thanks and nosed into the opening. Well, almost. Just as I hit the accelerator, a gas-sucking orangey-yellow monstrosity of a Hummer whipped over in front of me, very nearly shaving off the nose of my beloved Honda Fit. Shoeboxes tumbled from the passenger seat into the front floorboard, disgorging an array of summer heels and sandals. The guy hauling the glass looked at me, shrugged his shoulders, and kept going.

Creeping along with one eye forward and one eye on my side mirror (no easy feat), I kept my ever-hopeful blinker flashing. The driver of a semi soon motioned me over in front of him. *Thank you, Lord.*

7:37. For the umpteenth time since pulling onto I-65, I prayed for a break in the traffic. I was maneuvering the recently improved zone of terror once known as Malfunction Junction – the confluence of Interstates 65, 20, and 59 – and had made it across three lanes of traffic so I could switch to 20/59 and crawl my way toward downtown Birmingham. My next magical feat was to battle my way to the on-ramp for the Red Mountain Expressway and beeline it to the TV station.

I guess I should have started with that little tidbit. I'm the Bargainomics Lady on WEEE TV. Our slogan is "WEEE: we put the Entertainment in television!" On the first and third Thursday of every month, I make the morning drive from my tiny town of Caufield Corner into Birmingham, a.k.a. B-ham, for my five minutes of fame, telling viewers of the morning show, *It's a New Day, Alabama!*, where they can find the best bargains on the internet and locally, and occasionally throwing in other snippets of time- and money-saving wisdom.

After my segment, I run errands, shop, or occasionally have an early lunch before returning to the station for my next five minutes of fame during the noon news program. At least, that's my first and third Thursday routine. Every Thursday I do the noon news, but, thankfully, I'm only in rush hour traffic twice a month.

In B-ham, the worst of the bumper-to-bumper crawl generally occurs between seven and eight a.m., which explained why seeing 7:45 on my dash clock as I inched onto the final stretch was sending me into a tizzy – I or my empty chair would be live on the air at 8:00 a.m.

7:52. Shooting down the off ramp, I made the light onto 21st Avenue and maintained a cool and careful 35 up to and through the last light before turning into Vulcan Park and roaring uphill toward the gates of the station.

The solemn face of Vulcan, Roman god of the forge, greeted me as I steered toward the first big curve on the mountainside. Birmingham's huge, iron, bare-butted statue (known as the "moon over Homewood" to the neighboring city's residents who see his backside) has stood here since the 1930s. At fifty-six feet tall, he symbolizes Birmingham's roots in the iron and steel industry and holds the record as the largest cast iron statue in the world.

7:54. I screeched to a halt at the gate, let my window down, and jammed a finger on the call button. An electronic crackle on the speaker preceded the front desk's halt-who-goes-there spiel, which I rudely interrupted with, "It's me, Theresa," while hanging my head out the door so she can verify "Me's" identity in the camera.

The lift arm gate raised, and I launched the Fit forward, swerving into a vacant parking space near the front door. Bailing out, I dashed around the car, snatched open the passenger door, and threw the shoes – sans boxes – into the tote bag that at least

7

still held my segment notes.

7:56. Bounding up the front steps, I heard the door lock release before I even grabbed the handle. Opening it, I skidded across the floor and reached for the pen by the sign-in sheet. Sainted, dark-haired Theresa, the receptionist, waved me on. "Go!" she commanded. "I'll sign you in."

"I owe you!" I called back as I sprinted up the carpeted stairway.

7:57. A very anxious cameraman, Kevin, poked his head into the hallway, headset black against his mahogany skin. "You've got two minutes," he informed me, holding up a pair of slender fingers.

"Two minutes!" I marveled. "That means I have time to touch up my lip liner."

7:59. Scurried into the studio. Dumped the shoes onto the desk; then arranged them into a neat row facing the cameras. Slid into the seat next to Janice, the anchorwoman, plopped down my notes, and clipped on my mic, making a quick check to ensure the cord was hidden.

"Ten seconds," Kevin announced.

8:00 a.m. "Hi, and we're live in the studio with Judy Woodward Bates, our very own Bargainomics Lady," Janice beamed into the camera. Then, turning her attention to *moi*, she added, "What are you going to tell us about today?"

"Well, Janice," I began, "I've found a local store with one of the best shoe sales ever!" Out of the corner of my eye, I watched as Mickey, our prankster weather guy and cohost, eased behind the bank of cameras. Suddenly two puppets appeared and began to silently but passionately lip-lock. I've gotta hand it to Mickey – he's absolutely brilliant when it comes to creative distractions.

Janice, also catching the behind-the-cameras show, locked eyes with me in a silent "We'll get through this" as Kevin filled our viewers' screens with a shot of my shoe bargains.

"And finally, the regular price for these adorable flats by BC was fifty dollars, but I got them for only $4.99. I'm talking 90 percent off."

"The name of that shop again is Shoe Village," Janice interjected, sliding one hand out of sight beneath the desk and making a discreet circling motion with one finger to tell me the producer was yelling in her ear to wrap things up.

The store name appeared at the bottom of the monitor, so I knew the viewers were getting a look at the information. "That's it, Janice, at 336 West Andalusia Street in the Garden Grove Shopping Center," I responded, watching the address drop in underneath the store name.

Picking up speed as I saw Kevin giving a signal to hurry, I practically made one word out of my closing sentence: "And you can see all this info on the WEEE TV page of my website, Bargainomics.com."

"And we're out." Kevin's voice let us know we were no longer on camera.

Everybody in the studio burst out laughing as we watched Mickey continue his impromptu puppet show. He was in rare form, and I knew the audience was in for a treat when the commercial break ended.

Sure enough, the lanky, tanned, and silver-haired Mickey opened the weather with a brilliant smile, a gleam of mischief in his sparkling blue-gray eyes, and a puppet on each hand. Alternately, he delivered his report in a squeaky feminine voice as the girl puppet and a pretty impressive James Earl Jones imitation as the boy. When he announced the high for the day as 98, the boy puppet snuggled against the girl and murmured, "A heat wave, baby. Just like my love for you."

No wonder the guy – Mickey, that is – was so popular. Even at the height of summer when the weather is basically heat, heat, and more heat, he had a way of making his weather segments anything but boring and everything but predictable. Like my life.

3

8:07. I was off the clock, or at least not due back at the station until WEEE Know the News at high noon. At the front desk, I thanked Theresa again, signed myself out, and handed her my notes so she'd have the shoe info for viewers who called in saying they didn't catch all the details. Yes, they could have looked it up online, but not everyone wants to go to that much effort, and then there are some folks who still don't use the internet, poor things. I can't even imagine.

At a far more leisurely pace, I tossed the shoes into the hatch, climbed behind the wheel, and headed for Millie's, a half-hour drive northwest of B-ham and a million miles away from anything remotely citified. Millie and her husband, Bill, live in a rambling old farmhouse hidden at the end of a winding red dirt drive that's hardly more than a cart path through a forest of oak, pine, and hickory trees.

Turning in, I fervently wished Bill would cut back a tad of the over-burgeoning flora as I scraped through the masses of seven-bark (wild hydrangea) and beautyberry. Don't get me wrong – the place is gorgeous. But please, make room for humans. And their vehicles.

Standing sentinel was their mailbox, one of Millie's countless creations. Painted and festooned to look like a bizarre oblong head, the top of the box had been hammered down to form an inset trench which currently sprouted a full head of spiky green grass "hair." The door had been painted as a face with a wide-open mouth and a dangling pink tongue.

A round neck attached the mailbox head to a body decked out in well-worn denim overalls and finished off with a pair of shabby low-top work boots. Arms clad in a faded red shirt extended to hands resting gently against each side. Our carpenter grandfather, Papa Woodward, might not have recognized himself in Millie's metal art, but in spite of the weird head and punk hairdo, everyone in the family had immediately known who it represented as soon as they saw it.

On the opposite side of the drive, two tall, slender iron leaves shot from a four-foot curvy metal stem topped by a one-dimensional tulip head that served as the sign for Millie's business. Hand-painted in bright blue flowing script across both sides of the giant yellow blossom was: "Millicent's Studio – open by chance or appointment." Millie sure knew how to literally make an entrance.

Once I'd cleared the gauntlet, the farmhouse came into view. Scattered around it in easy walking distance was Millie's studio, the barn, the old smokehouse, the spring house, the pump house, and the original family outhouse – a two-seater, just so you'll know we come from a wealthy background.

The farmhouse is a 1,600-square-foot single story with white-painted cedar siding, a silver tin roof, and a covered porch stretching all the way across the front. No shutters. A single stone chimney on the end facing away from the driveway.

Papa's granddaddy, Josiah, was the first Woodward to settle on this forty-acre spread, and he built the original two-room structure in the mid-1800s when the Woodwards moved from Crawford County, Georgia over into Alabama. Papa's daddy, Lafayette, had added on two more rooms, and Papa (Robert Lee) had eventually added three more, including a bathroom with an elephant trunk toilet and a solid oak wall tank.

For those of you who aren't up on your toilet trivia, an elephant trunk toilet has a bowl that looks like the lower half of an elephant's head. The drain is in the front instead of the back of the bowl bottom and shapes the base like a front-facing elephant head, trunk and all. With the tank high on the wall and the lovely brass pull chain, it really is a thing of beauty. So, yes, I admit it. When it comes to that bathroom, I am one of many who suffer from toilet envy.

A 400-square-foot sharecropper's cabin had been converted into the studio and tiny showroom for Millie's paintings, sculptures, and pottery. I putted past the farmhouse at a crawl, watching for the kittens of the barn cat, Matilda.

Named for our great-grandmother, Lafayette's wife, and her proclivity for reproduction – she'd borne sixteen little Woodwards – the feline Matilda was pretty impressive, too. She'd spit out eight kittens in her first and only shot at motherhood.

Speaking of shot, that's what Millie had wanted to do to the big bruiser of a tomcat appropriately named Rover who'd assaulted poor Matilda shortly after Millie had rescued her from certain death. The emaciated young tortoiseshell was licking some litterbug's McDonald's wrapper when Millie spotted her on Highway 78 and whipped into the nearest break in the median, leaped out, scooped up the little furball, and rushed her to a vet.

The half-grown kitten was bathed and de-parasited, and Millie was told to bring her in for spaying once she was in better physical condition. Poor creature, as she was recuperating in a comfy bed of fresh straw, Rover roamed over from the neighboring farm, crept into the barn, and had his way with his weak and helpless victim. Just writing about it makes me want to stomp his tail off.

Anyway, the kitten, who was thus far nameless, handled her teenage pregnancy like a trouper, filled out, filled up, and shocked us all with the birth of eight healthy, adorable babies. True enough, three of them looked like their father – long gray fur with what will probably become yellow eyes – but who can hold that against them? They're all so precious. The mom's spectacular aplomb earned her the honor of being named Matilda.

14

Footnote here. Rover's owners, the Bollings, the neighbors at the next farm over, were given a choice: neuter your monster or we'll do it for you – without anesthesia and with a dull knife. The Bollings had Rover at the vet the next day, and Rover's roving days are over. Or at least, shall we say, no longer reproductive.

No kittens darted from under the porch or bushes, so I continued easing forward. Suddenly a loud mournful half-bark, half-howl erupted from only inches away, and I simultaneously slammed on the brakes and jumped like I'd been zapped with a cattle prod. Bo, short for Jethro Bodine from the TV classic *The Beverly Hillbillies*, a three-legged bloodhound, was right outside my window. Taking my stop to be rolling out the welcome mat, Bo leapt up on the side of the car, balancing with ease on his one back leg.

"Down!" I commanded, lowering my window so he could hear me. Bo's head lunged through the opening, immediately adorning my formerly clean khaki capris with a long string of slobber. His tongue stretched outward, straining to give my neck and face a mucilaginous (that's like slimy or slobbery) greeting.

Switching off the engine, I opened the door just enough to release the latch, made a lightning-fast grab for Bo's front paws, and held them through the window as I slowly climbed out of the vehicle. "I'm glad to see you, too, Bo," I spoke into the big brown eyes. As soon as I was standing, I gave Bo's paws a little backward push and let go. With this practiced maneuver, my car escaped without Bo's toenails scraping down the door and with only one set of paw prints and a few slobber patches left behind. Bo dropped nonchalantly back on all threes.

The trick with Bo, I'd learned, was like driving: always keep at least one hand on the wheel – or in this case, the dog. Pet his head. Scratch his ears. But do something to keep his paws on the ground. Otherwise, the drool on my pants would be butkus compared to what he could do with my whole outfit within paw and tongue reach.

So, with my torso tilted lopsided and one hand busily patting Bo, I shuffled my way to the front stoop of Millie's workshop. The door swung open and doting Bo forgot my existence as the love of his life made her appearance.

"How's my sugar dumplin' sweetie boy?" Millie baby-talked the big hound as she stooped to hug him. Bo, overcome with emotion, wagged his tail so hard that his whole body joined in.

"Oh, yeah, right," I snorted. "You're wearing armor." I was referring to the oversized paint-spattered smock protecting her from Bo's barrage of affection.

"Just listen to her, Bo-Bo," Millie prattled on, addressing only Mr. Three-Legs. "Aunt Judy doesn't like your kisses. But I do! Yes, I do, you little angel." Bo all but swooned at her feet on that last line.

"Hey, I love animals, but please, I'm not his aunt!"

"Well, alrighty, then," Millie returned, rising and pushing open the door to her studio.

"Are you ready to go?" I asked, following her inside and

shutting the pooch out of our conversation.

"Just about," she answered. "Let me wash my hands and lose this smock."

That's one of the (but I haven't told you about the rest of them – yet) things about Millie that irritates the tee-tee out of me. She can roll out of bed at 6 a.m., whip up a full course breakfast for Bill (I have a husband, too – Larry, whom I'll tell you about later), pat on a little makeup, run a comb through her hair, and throw on whatever she finds and come out looking like a movie star. I kid you not.

Today's number was a fuchsia pink cotton knit twin set – a tank and short-sleeved jacket – with white capris and silver sandals. And perfectly matching fuchsia nail polish on her fingernails and toenails. And absolutely darling white J-hoop earrings. I refuse to describe the double-stranded white shell bracelet and necklace.

You know, I'm the one on TV. I'm the one who gets recognized everywhere I go. And yet my Sophia Loren-doubling cousin takes zero effort to look like a million bucks while I have to work my fanny off to come in a passable, but paltry, second.

Even losing her hair during radiation and chemotherapy didn't diminish her beauty. She could wrap a scarf around that bald head and pass for exotic royalty. And when her baby fine, straight, dark hair departed, the new batch came in lusciously thick and platinum silver with a teensy bit of darker streaking. No hair stylist could have done the spectacular work that God did.

I'm not saying I'm jealous, mind you. It just gets so darn aggravating to be constantly upstaged by someone who is always: (1) complaining about her looks; (2) wishing she could lose weight; and (3) thinking I have more talent than she does. Puh-leeeeze! Millie's pinky could outshine any ten-fingered attempt I'll ever make at anything.

It's always cracked up both of us when people ask if we're sisters. We can't figure why anyone would think that. She's bigger-boned than me; an inch or two taller – about five foot three; and has the dark skin and brown eyes that come from our grandmother's Creek and Cherokee ancestry. Only a little exposure to the sun and she looks coffee bean brown and even more of a head-turner.

Me, I take after my mom's Scotch-Irish side of the family. I'm not quite five foot two; no eyes of blue (in case you remember the song) – well, sort of blue-green – and my hair leans toward Fiery Sunset in summer and Spicy Cedar in winter. In some form or another, I have reddish-brown hair. What's underneath that, only my hair stylist knows for sure. Actually, she doesn't know, either, since I color my own, and she only does my haircuts.

I haven't seen my natural hair color since early high school – I was a bleached blonde my junior and senior years. Best I can recall, and based on ancient photos, my hair was a dark chestnut with lots of red highlights. I kind of got the scraps of my mother's beautiful auburn hair. Mother couldn't have missed being a redhead. Her dad was auburn-haired and her mom had the fire

18

engine red that matched her temperament.

Naturally, my Celtic predecessors also blessed me with milk white skin that would rather burn than tan and a smattering of arm and leg (no facial) freckles, which are now indistinguishable from my age spots. And while Millie got her perfect white teeth from Mother Nature, I got my pearly whites from orthodontics.

Still, I didn't look too bad today. My short spiky, freshly applied Fiery Sunset red hair was holding its own in spite of the humidity. My bright blue jacket went well with my multi-colored pullover; the top added just enough taupe into the mix to pull the khaki cropped pants and jacket together as an outfit. But when I'd walked out the door of the TV station, the early morning sun had already begun baking the inside of my car, so the jacket and I had parted company. So there I stood, upstaged as always.

A mile or so from Blue Creek Park, Ray John Fitzhugh stood outside the luxury car, cradling his head and rocking on the balls of his feet, his eyes wild with fear. "I hit him hard. Real hard. I mighta killed him!"

"And still you fail to deliver as instructed." The Collector held out his empty hands and shook his head disapprovingly.

"I'll get it, I swear I will." Ray John leaned in the back window and attempted a look of confidence. "I got there as quick as I could. There weren't supposed to be nobody in there. And besides," he added, his voice quaking despite his attempt at bravado, "if that thang is worth all this much trouble, I might oughta be gettin' a little more money."

"Kill him," The Collector instructed his chauffeur as nonchalantly as ordering the swatting of an insect.

Electrified by terror, Ray John broke into a run, feet flying across the open field, and crashing into the undergrowth. A hulking form climbed from the driver's seat, slipping on gloves as he did so.

"This shouldn't take long, sir," the driver said, smiling as he nodded to his employer. Extracting a coil of narrow wire from his pocket, the giant sprinted with surprising ease into the forest, following the clearly blazed trail of his panicking quarry.

"Okay," Millie said, lifting a deep cardboard box and shoving it toward me, "you carry this one and I think I can manage the other."

"Oh, no, you don't," I retorted. "Not until I wash some of Bo's slobber off my pants."

Ducking behind a trio of bi-fold doors Millie had transformed into a colorful room divider and display wall, I stepped around and over boxes of supplies and stacks of crates repurposed as shipping containers for Millie's creations. A big plastic laundry sink we'd gotten for nearly nothing at a salvage store's tent sale (because the legs had been missing) stood on crutches – yes, honest-to-goodness wooden crutches Bill had cut off and transformed into sink supports – near a long narrow window, years of paint spattering every surface with a myriad of colors.

Snatching a paper towel from the wall-mounted dispenser, I slapped the faucet away from a jar of paint brushes, turned it on, and wet my paper towel. Rubbing lightly, I was hopeful Bo's slobber spots would disappear and the water spots manage to dry before we got to the gallery.

Oh, I failed to cover that point. The whole reason I was at Millie's this morning was to help her take a load of figurines to Art in the Park, one of the two local galleries where Millie's work is carried and, I might add, flies off the shelves at a very profitable pace.

The shop is located at the south corner of Blue Creek Park and owned by local artist Art Molina, a potter whose contemporary face jugs have become wildly popular. I was shocked and thrilled when Larry gave me one for our anniversary last year – a single jug with two side-by-side faces, one a heavy-browed male and the other a wire-eyelashed female.

"I think it all came off," I called as I tossed the paper towel into the trash and crossed to the stainless steel table opposite the sink wall where a glittering fairy sat perched atop a lifelike mushroom.

I paused at the showroom side of the room divider and admired a pair of oval-framed watercolors that I didn't recall seeing before. "Nice," I nodded to Millie. "When'd you do these?"

"I didn't," Millie beamed. "Look who signed them."

"Niki!" I exclaimed. "Well, I shouldn't be surprised." Niki was Millie's eight-year-old granddaughter. I had a photo of her at age two wearing a tam and artist's smock and standing beside an easel displaying one of her first finger-painting masterpieces.

"I'm just plain thrilled," Millie responded, wresting the door open with one box-laden hand. "Let's get to Art's and I'll treat you to brunch at Dupree's afterwards."

"Deal!" I said. "Just remember I have to be back at the station by noon." Between the time crunch and the offer of Dupree's, I was highly motivated. In less than a minute, the Fit was on its way back to the city.

One of the oldest restaurants in town, Dupree's fronted a cobblestone alleyway and offered outdoor dining in a brick-paved courtyard surrounded by an ancient ornamental wrought iron fence smothered in English ivy and overhung with huge oaks and magnolias. A three-tiered black cast iron fountain centered the courtyard, and its gentle noises mingled with the rustling leaves to create the only music needed for entertainment.

The inside eating areas and kitchen were housed in the basement level of one of B-ham's old Southside mansions not too far from Blue Creek Park. The front of the house faced busy Avalon Street and contained the offices of law firm Wilburn, Payne, and Dupree. Back in the 1950s, New Orleans native Hilda Dupree, wife of Oliver Dupree, persuaded her husband and his partners to let her renovate their building's basement and try her hand as a restauranteur.

Soon *The Birmingham News* proclaimed Dupree's as "Southern comfort food with a New Orleans flair." The reputation and the menu had stuck. Serving variations on French, Creole, Cajun, and Southern home cooking, the place enjoys continual popularity with young, old, and in-between.

"Lobster omelet," I fairly drooled as I took the off ramp for Blue Creek Parkway. One of Dupree's signature dishes, it's loaded with fresh lobster, cream cheese, brie, and diced tomatoes, and covered in a luscious light cream sauce.

"Heavenly," agreed Millie. "How about we split the omelet and order the Bananas Foster pancakes?"

"Perfect!" I practically sang. Fluffy buttermilk pancakes layered with sliced bananas and chopped pecans, smothered in warm Bananas Foster sauce, and topped with homemade whipped cream. If we died during brunch, it'd be with smiles on our faces.

Art in the Park was a flat-roofed, single-story structure with a sandstone front and windowless concrete block sides. On either side of the front door, two substantial picture windows were filled with displays. Above the doorway hung the building's original classic TV-shaped sign. "Art in the Park" now replaced the neon "Radio & TV Repair" across the screen, and the surrounding cabinetry, knobs, and legs were painted in a brilliant array of stripes and polka dots.

"Pull around back," Millie instructed. "All the artists have to check their work in through the storeroom."

Cruising past the front door parking spaces, I eased through the side lot and nosed into the alley behind the building. A dull gray metal door stood half open and faded stick-on lettering identified it as "Deliveries."

"Go ahead and get out," I told Millie. "Then I can pull close to the building and leave enough space for traffic to get by."

At this, Millie bailed out and waited for me to park. Mission accomplished, I exited the car and popped the hatch so we could each grab a box of figurines.

Balancing a load in one hand, I slammed the hatch and fumbled for the lock button on my key. That done, I followed Millie's lead into Art's storeroom.

"Hey, Art!" Millie called as she stepped through the open doorway. "Where's the light switch?"

No answer.

"Here it is," I mumbled through a face full of box as I flipped a switch and eased my cargo onto a wooden table spanning the nearest wall. A momentary hum and pause and fluorescent light fixtures blinked to life across the ceiling. Millie settled her box next to mine and hurried over to a side door marked "Potty."

"I can't believe you have to go again already," I griped. "Didn't you go right before we left your studio?"

"Oh, excuse me," Millie retorted, hand on doorknob. "I forgot this was your day to monitor my bladder. And," she added as she leaned into the door, "for your information, this isn't the bathroom. It's the room for Art's potter's wheel." She shoved the door inward. "Huh. He's not in here, either."

"He's probably with a customer," I suggested, crossing to an unmarked door that opened into Art's showroom. A quick glance confirmed we were the only two folks in the building.

"Maybe he went out the front while we were parking in back," Millie proposed. But when she reached the front door, we both spotted the "Open" sign still turned inward and the deadbolt clearly in place.

"This is too weird," Millie mused. "I talked to Art last night and told him I'd be here first thing this morning. And even if he had an errand to run, why would he leave the back door standing open?"

"I think you just solved the mystery," I said. "He probably ran across to the market and left the back door open so you wouldn't have to wait on him to let you in."

"I bet that's it," Millie concurred. "He'll probably walk in any minute now."

But ten minutes later, we were still waiting on the illusive Art. And my stomach was starting to growl. Visions of Dupree's lobster omelet were making the rumblings worse.

"Look," I advised, "leave Art a note, tell him where we left the boxes, and let's go on to Dupree's. We can check back afterwards."

Millie arched one eyebrow and gave me her I'm-not-messin'-with-you look. "There is no way I'm leaving my stuff until Art's standing here to hand me a receipt for every piece of it."

"Fine," I grumped. "Might as well borrow his bathroom while we wait."

"And you want to criticize *my* bladder?" Millie returned, pointing to the door we'd just come through. "Look to the right as soon as you walk in. Red door in the corner."

Following her directions, I found the bathroom, took care of business, and started back to the showroom. That's when I saw the spots on the floor.

27

"Uh, Mil," I called out. "You better c'mere."

Millie walked up behind me and let out a soft gasp. "Are you thinking what I'm thinking?" Millie whispered.

"If you're thinking that's blood, I am," I answered.

Backtracking across the storeroom, we located what looked like the initial blood spatter. (We're not crime scene investigators, but we do watch the shows.) A fist-sized patch of sticky reddish-brown was smeared by a partial shoeprint.

"Let's not get crazy here," I cautioned. "Maybe Art got hurt and simply drove himself to the emergency room and, in the rush, forgot to close the back door."

"Not likely," Millie responded. "Art only lives a couple blocks from here, and he either walks or rides his bike unless the weather's terrible. If he was okay enough to go home to get his car, he'd have remembered to lock up."

"OK, so let's see where the blood drops lead and then decide whether or not we should call the police. I mean, it's blood, for sure, but it's not like there's a ton of it. And it's still wet, so whatever happened couldn't have been long ago."

We each stood to one side of the blood trail and took a few cautious steps. Suddenly Millie threw up a hand and halted us like some sort of professional tracker.

"Don't move," she whispered, pointing behind me. "I see more bloody partial footprints. If somebody attacked Art, these may help us identify his assailant." (Her use of the word *assailant* was a sure indicator that she was in full CSI mode.)

I did a slow and cautious one-eighty and rolled my eyes in disbelief. "Great going, Sherlock," I hissed, lifting one of my sandaled feet. "The prints are mine. I must have stepped in the edge of that blob when I came out of the bathroom."

"Well, that's just dandy," Millie huffed. "You know better than to tamper with evidence!"

"Evidence!" I fairly shrieked. "We don't even know if a crime's been committed! And if you will recall, I was the one who noticed the blood in the first place!"

"Oh, don't get your knickers in a twist," Millie returned. "Let's keep following the trail and see where he went."

A smeared zigzag of droplets continued out the door and into the alley. As we crossed the narrow pavement, weeds choked the roadside, but a freshly trampled patch of clover seemed to indicate Art had headed down the low embankment into the woods. A few yards beyond the trees we could see the meandering walking path of Blue Creek Park.

"Maybe he saw someone on the pathway and went there to get help," I proposed. "Let's hit the trail and see if we spot him. You go left and I'll go right."

We plunged into the low growth, watching not only for blood drops, but also poison oak, poison ivy, poison sumac, and poisonous snakes – all with which we're abundantly blessed in Alabama. I picked my way around a lethal patch of blackberry brambles and soon lost sight of Millie.

By the time I thrashed my way to the walking path, I looked like an escapee from a "Survivor" episode. My once clean khakis had green smears from the honeysuckle vines I'd struggled through, and the hem of my top had been snagged and pulled loose on one side. Add the twigs in my hair, the scratches and squashed mosquitoes on my face and ankles, and the swarm of gnats around my head, and you have a pretty good idea of how much my appearance had taken a turn for the worse.

Millie chose that moment to hurry toward me, hair perfectly coiffed and not a gnat, mosquito, twig, or mark on her. (I'm telling you, there's something creepy wrong about how she manages this.) The only thing out of place was the fact that the minute I spotted her, she turned her back on me and took off in the direction she'd come from.

"Hey, wait up!" I yelled. "Where are you going?"

"It's Art. In the park!" she called back over her shoulder. "Come quick!"

"You mean we need to go back to the shop?" I bellowed at her vanishing backside.

"No! I mean, it's Art – in the park. I've found him!"

As we stooped beside the crumpled form of Art Molina, relief and concern hammered us as he groaned the words, "Please help me."

"I've already called 9-1-1," Millie informed both me and Art, her cell phone still clutched in one shaking hand.

"Just lie still and EMTs will be here in no time," I added.

"I-I think I'm okay," Art rasped, levering himself upward.

Seeing his insistence, Millie and I each grabbed an arm and helped him into a sitting position. His normally immaculate slacks and polo shirt were matted with blood, dirt, and brambles.

"May need a few stitches in the back of your head," Millie told him. He winced as his hand touched a patch of his sandy brown, blood-caked hair.

Gently I separated the mat to get a look at the lump and gash beneath it. "Yep," I nodded. "I'd say you're gonna need several stitches."

"And you may have a concussion, too," Millie frowned. "Art, how in the world did this happen?"

"I'd walked to work and was about to use my key when I noticed the doorframe was bent in around the catch for the door lock. I eased the door open and slipped inside. Next thing I knew, some guy shoved me in the back hard enough to knock me to my knees. Before I could get up, he whacked me in the head. I hit the floor like a sack of potatoes."

"So how did you wind up out here?" I asked.

"I chased after him. While I was on the floor, I heard him rummaging around in the shop – sure hope he didn't break anything – and then he went running by me and out the back. He ran into the park and I tried to follow, but before I'd gone very far, I got really dizzy and I guess I passed out."

"What'd he take?" Millie questioned.

"I don't know," Art shrugged. "I didn't see anything in his hands."

"Maybe," I suggested, "he took cash and stuffed it in his pants pockets. What was he wearing?"

"I know the police will love hearing me say this, but it's true. It all happened so fast, I'm really not sure. It was a dark hoodie – black or navy – and he had the hood pulled up to where I really couldn't see his face."

Art paused, collected his thoughts, and continued. "He was dark-skinned…"

"Like African-American, you mean?" Millie interrupted.

"No, like tanned. Tall and skinny. And fast. He ran like he'd been shot out of a cannon."

"He'd have to be fast to outrun you," I told him. Art had been competing in local marathons for years and had recently taken first place in the Rump Shaker 5K, an annual event to raise funds for and increase awareness of colorectal cancer.

The sirens grew louder and, within moments, a white van with a bar of flashing red lights across the top and "JeffCo EMS" emblazoned on the sides came jolting across the park, a flashing and wailing police car right behind it. Millie and I waved and pointed to Art. As if they wouldn't figure out it's the bloody guy on the ground who needs their attention.

Seconds later, the sirens were silent and the paramedics were tending to Art. Two Birmingham police officers – Officer Stanford and Detective Metz, according to their quick introductions – stood to one side. It was like looking at salt and pepper. Stanford was truly the whitest white guy I'd ever seen – skin paler than mine, close-cropped white blonde hair, and icy blue eyes that made me wonder if he was wearing colored contacts.

Detective Metz, on the other hand, was the color of a Dove milk chocolate candy bar – my personal favorite. His perfectly shaped bald head sat atop a thick short neck sprouting from a linebacker-sized body that was clearly kept in great shape. His eyes casually swept over my Wild Woman of Borneo look and he immediately addressed his questions to Mrs. Neat Freak. "Ma'am, can you tell us what happened?"

"Well, Judy came by my studio this morning right after she left the TV station. You may recognize her from WEEE TV – she's the Bargainomics Lady," Millie began.

"If I might interject, Detective," I said, plucking a stray honeysuckle blossom from my hair and twirling it between my

34

thumb and finger. "I believe, cousin dear," I offered, smiling sweetly at Millie, "that they'd like to know what happened to Art, not hear an account of our entire morning."

"Well, excuuuuuse me!" Millie huffed. "I was merely trying to be thorough."

Ignoring Millie's crossed arms and glare, I offered an unadorned version of our arrival at Art's and our subsequent tracking of the blood drops that led us to find him. "And that," I concluded, "is when Millie called 9-1-1."

"Thank you, ma'am," Detective Metz responded. "Now if I could get both your names and addresses and contact numbers where we can reach you if we have any further questions."

"We can just give you our cards," I suggested, reaching for my handbag. "Our purses!" I yelped. "They're in the storeroom at Art's, and the door's standing wide open!"

"Stanford," Detective Metz turned to his partner, "you wanna head on up there and check things out? As soon as I get a statement from the vic here, I'll join you at the shop."

"Will do," Stanford nodded and began trudging through the underbrush toward the alleyway.

"And we're gonna take Mr. Molina over to UAB Hospital and get his head examined," one EMT grinned as they loaded Art into the back of the ambulance.

"Don't worry about the shop, Art," I called before the doors were slammed shut. "Millie and I will check things out and lock up for you. Then we'll meet you at the hospital."

8

A short time later on a rutted dirt road, the sleek dark car unhurriedly bumped along. Halting by a roadside ravine, the driver released the trunk lid and reached into the glove compartment. Extracting a pair of blue disposable shoe covers, he slid them over his Italian leather loafers and exited the car. Moving to the trunk, he lifted his cargo, grunted slightly, and placed the tarp-wrapped bundle near the edge of the drop-off. His gloved hands gave a push and the package rolled and bounced its way to the bottom.

Nodding his satisfaction, he returned to the car and removed his shoe covers, neatly tucking them, and then his gloves, into a zippered plastic bag that would soon be nothing but ashes.

I dropped Millie at the emergency room doors and burned rubber toward the TV station. My tramp through the bushes hadn't exactly done wonders for my appearance, but a few minutes at the makeup mirror and I was once again passably human. As soon as my noontime segment wrapped, I was out the door and on my way back to the hospital.

It took ten stitches to close the gash on the back of Art's head. Thankfully, there was no concussion, but he'd have plenty of bruises and soreness from hitting the storeroom floor. Considering what he'd been through, Art was in miraculously good shape, and Millie and I both sent up prayers of thanksgiving.

I pulled the car to the emergency room doors, and Millie led Art and his wheelchair-pushing aide to where I was waiting. Easing Art into the front passenger seat, Millie helped him with his seat belt before hopping in back.

"Where to first, Art?" I asked, noticing the prescription atop the stack of papers in his lap.

"Tomlin's," he said, referring to the pharmacy next door to his shop. "My head's splitting, or split, I should say" – he managed a weak smile – "and the doc assured me this med will help with the pain and swelling."

"Done," I nodded, and pulled into traffic.

A half hour later, Art wobbled through his shop, Millie supporting one side and me the other. "Looks like he didn't even go into the showroom," Art mused. "Maybe he broke into the wrong place. I mean, what if he was messed up on drugs and thought this was the pharmacy's back door?"

"It's certainly possible," I concurred, "but you still need to look around back here and see if there's anything at all different."

"Aside from the blood," Millie added unnecessarily.

"There's just so little back here worth stealing," Art murmured, poking his head into the Potty. "I know I need to give this place a good going-over, but I've got to lie down, ladies. I'll come back in the morning and take a better look around when my head's not so foggy."

"Oh, Art, you poor thing," I apologized. "We'll drive you home right now. Do you want us to run across to the market and grab you a plate lunch?"

"Thanks," Art said as he stifled a yawn, "but all I can think of right now is putting my head on a pillow."

We got Art settled on his sofa and left his meds and a glass of water within easy reach on the coffee table. As soon as he had fallen asleep, we let ourselves out and made a beeline for the Silver Express. Dupree's would have to wait till another day, but the Silver Express was not exactly deprivation. Housed in a gleaming silver former train car, its reputation had been built on downhome cooking, and no patron could possibly leave there hungry or disappointed.

"What're you gonna order?" Millie asked. "I'm thinking about a vegetable plate."

"That does sound good," I agreed. "What's our coupon good for?"

"It's a BOGO," Millie answered, waving the buy one, get one free offer she'd clipped from a local magazine. "If you'll share your plate, I'll share mine."

The next few minutes were filled with nothing but background noises and an occasional "Mmmm" as we feasted on collard greens, baked sweet potatoes, creamed corn, fried green tomatoes, fried okra, and speckled butter beans. We flagged down our waitress and placed take-out orders for Bill and Larry. Who wanted to cook after what we'd just eaten?

Creeping ever watchfully up Millie's drive, the farmhouse came into view and I spotted Bill ensconced in one of the porch rockers with a giant glass of iced tea in one hand and Bo beside him, shaking himself from what was probably his fifteenth nap of the day to greet the returning Adored One. Bill, having shed the business suit his day job required, was wearing his favorite well-worn overalls and straw hat.

In his office duds, this studious-looking bespectacled guy could pass for an uptown lawyer and yet, throw on the overalls, and he totally fit the part of a regular ol' country farmer. And farm, he could. Bill's green thumb was appreciated by friends, family, neighbors, coworkers, and fellow church members, all of whom benefited from his labor of love in his massive garden.

"Better make a run for it," Millie warned as she stepped from the car. "Bill's picked a bushel of squash, and he's looking for somebody to pass it off on."

"Any other time I'd love to have it," I laughed, "but tomorrow is already booked with helping Art, and Saturday, Larry and I hope to make a run up to the lake if we can manage it."

"I'll meet you at Art's house in the morning," Millie promised. "Is 9:30 early enough?"

"Make it 9:00 and I'll bring along some croissants for breakfast."

9

As Larry polished off his meal from Silver Express, he and I relaxed in front of the TV, watching the evening news. News anchor Steve Cofer wore a solemn face as he announced to the camera, "Thank you for watching the Thursday evening edition of WEEE News. This just in from our news team out in Veramosa. The body of a local man has been found near the Glaze Creek landfill. Melanie, what can you tell us about this?"

The studio disappeared and reporter Melanie Posten came into view, a multitude of police and emergency vehicles in the background, lights flashing. I had a lot of admiration for Melanie; nobody could do a better job of looking good under adverse conditions. Her deep burgundy silk suit set the perfect tone for such a somber report while looking elegant enough for a meeting with the governor. And those shoes! I'd have to find out where she bought them.

"Well, Steve," Melanie began, "I'm standing near the site where the body of a man police have identified as Raymond John

Fitzhugh of Chalybeate Springs was found only a short time ago. According to Veramosa Police Chief Mitchell Patterson, Fitzhugh had been nearly decapitated and his tarp-wrapped body subsequently dumped at this location. There are no suspects at the present time, but as Chief Patterson wants me to make very clear, the investigation has just begun, and he's sure they'll be adding new information as the evening progresses."

"How horrible!" I remarked. "I wonder what sort of person this Fitzhugh guy was."

As if in answer to my question, Steve tossed a question at Melanie: "Do we know anything else about the victim?"

"Hang on one second, Steve," Melanie yelled above the din of a siren-screeching patrol car. One hand on her microphone, she jammed the other against her ear, struggling to hear Steve's voice through her earpiece.

The siren faded, and Melanie tried again. "We've learned that Raymond John Fitzhugh was better known as Ray John and had a lengthy record for petty crimes. His brother, Charles Fitzhugh, is the owner of Superior Cadillac and a respected member of several local business organizations. So far, we've been unable to reach Charles Fitzhugh for comment."

Friday morning. Larry was at his part-time job at his friend Terrell's Classic Garage where he and Terrell spent their days as happy as proverbial pigs in slop. Larry had retired at the ripe old age of forty-nine from his maintenance job at U.S. Steel and simply had to find a way to keep grease under his fingernails.

Working with Terrell for the past several years fulfilled that need and gave him hours of time amid some of the coolest cars on the planet. From Fords and Chevys to the occasional Studebaker or Hudson, a constant stream of fixer-uppers limped into Terrell's and left car-show ready. Larry has said more than once that he hopes there'll be mechanic work for him to do in heaven.

My early-riser hubby was up and gone two hours before I knew it was morning. When I made it as far as the kitchen, I found a freshly picked rose stuck in a water-filled Dr. Pepper bottle and a note that said: "Off to Terrell's. Coffee's ready – just hit the button. Muffins warming in the oven." As always, his note ended with "XOXO." Gives you some idea why our marriage has successfully passed the thirty-year mark.

Out on the screened porch with my coffee and muffin, I opened the large square door above a row of drawers in a rustic chifforobe resting against the solid wall of the house. Grabbing the remote to the small TV inside, I hit the "on" button and tuned in the morning show just in time for the news segment.

Janice Rodman stared into the camera, her big blue eyes serious as she read from the teleprompter. "Turning to local news, the body of murder victim Raymond John Fitzhugh was discovered around 5:00 p.m. yesterday evening near the Glaze Creek landfill in Veramosa. Our news team has been investigating this tragedy, and we've been able to locate Fitzhugh's last place of residence in Chalybeate Mobile Home Park. Reporter Marquita Richards spoke briefly with the victim's wife, Jewel Fitzhugh."

The scene was the doorway of a squalid travel trailer where a shapely female in skintight clothing and a pound of makeup leaned against the doorframe. "I've done told you people all I know to tell," Jewel Fitzhugh snapped, running a nervous hand over her really bad bleach job. The cigarette she clutched between her fingers curled smoke into the trailer.

"You have no idea who or why anyone would want to harm your husband?" Marquita asked, extending the microphone toward the woman. Marquita's sapphire blue outfit looked absolutely stunning.

"I don't know nothin' 'bout nothin'!" Jewel shouted, "and y'all best get outta here!"

Despite her tough talk, what I saw in Jewel's eyes was fear. Or maybe desperation.

10

Art looked a bit like a raccoon, but he seemed to be in good spirits. Either that, or his pain meds were doing an outstanding job.

"I've looked this place over top to bottom," Art declared to me and Millie, "and I can't find one thing missing or even out of place."

"OK, then let's start from the beginning," I told him. "What's come into this shop in the last few days?"

"Let me think a minute." Art paused, spinning in a slow circle inside the showroom. Joan Haas brought me those two pastels on Monday. Aren't they too gorgeous?"

"Does Joan give lessons?" Millie asked. "I'd love to know how she gets her dewdrops so realistic."

"Millie, you wear me out!" I shrieked. "Your worst day of painting beats Joan's best any day! You should be giving Joan lessons."

"Alrighty then," Millie shrugged. "And thanks, I guess." Turning back to Art, she added, "What else?"

"Well, Eric Johnson brought this metal art in Wednesday. I'm so glad I was one of the first studios to pick up his work. Every piece I've had in here has brought more money than the previous one."

Millie and I stared at the glistening four-foot stainless steel fish. Not exactly what either of us would want to take home, but I loved Eric's hummingbird piece that was now in my garden.

"What about the day before?" I questioned. "Did you get anything in on Tuesday?"

Art squeezed his lower lip between his thumb and forefinger, brows knitted. "No, not a thing." And then he snapped his fingers. "Wednesday evening! I totally forgot! When I locked up, I drove out to Carrie Parker's and picked up some of her clay pieces. Then I stopped back by and dropped them off. They're still in the storeroom."

Moving at a snail's pace, Art shuffled into the storeroom, explaining as he walked. "Carrie's one of my primitive artists. She does pit-fired pottery, and she's one of the best. Doesn't drive, though, and lives out in the absolute boonies on the Little Warrior River. Anyway, I picked up four of her latest pieces. Here, let me show you." He pulled a cardboard box to the front of the table.

Gently, Art lifted a newspaper-wrapped lump from one corner of the box. "Carrie digs her own clay right along the riverbank. She's one of a dying breed."

Art removed the paper and unveiled an orangey-brown clay urn smudged with black from the fire pit. A serpent coiled around the outside, but unlike any I'd seen before, part of the snake's body arched outward to form a handle, with the head flattened against the urn and its reptilian eyes staring malevolently.

"Fabulous!" Millie gushed, feeling the urn's smooth surface.

Art gingerly placed the urn on the counter and lifted a second piece from the box. It was a seated boy with tousled, charcoal-streaked hair, legs spraddled out and large feet sticking up in front. His backside was open, forming a bowl shape.

"'We are the clay, and thou our potter,'" I quoted from Isaiah 64:8. "I get it! He's a flowerpot."

"A folk-art planter," Art corrected, "which pays much more handsomely than a 'flower pot,' let me assure you."

Art placed the flower pot boy (he could call it whatever he wanted, but I knew a flower pot when I saw one) next to the urn and lifted out the third piece of Carrie Parker's creations, a pig-tailed girl that perfectly matched the boy pot.

"Irresistible," I enthused. "I want the pair, Art. Now make me flowerpot prices on these folk-art planters."

"On the house," Art answered. "A small price for my rescue yesterday." Turning to Millie, he added, "And if there's anything in the shop you have your eye on, it's yours."

Millie wiggled her eyebrows diabolically. "Within reason," Art qualified his previous offer. He smiled at both of us. "You'll never know how much I appreciate you two."

"As much as it pains me to turn down a free offer," I told him, "we decline." I pulled out my debit card and handed it over.

Millie nodded in agreement. "You might have to rescue us one day. Then we'll call it even."

As Art carefully rewrapped the boy planter, Millie ran her hands over the girl one. "This is just wonderful," she gushed. "Come to think of it, I met Mrs. Parker at the Kentuck Festival in Northport a few years ago. She was a lot younger than I'd expected. Nice lady."

"Yes, she is," agreed Art. "She's still in her forties and has already seen more troubles than most people endure in a lifetime, ninety percent of which came from her husband and daughter."

"What do you mean?" I queried.

"Mac Parker used to knock her around. Many a time I'd come by to pick up her work and she'd have a black eye or big bruise on her arm. She'd always tell me some lame story about walking into a door or taking a fall," Art explained. "And I might've believed her, except that most of it stopped the day they found him floating in the river. He'd gone out fishing and apparently fallen out of his boat – drunk, no doubt."

"Most of it?" Millie interjected. "You mean her daughter ...?"

"Hey, you didn't hear that from me," Art interrupted. "Jewel's a heavy drinker with a temper like her daddy's. Wouldn't surprise me if she was into drugs, too. The Parkers may have been white trash, but that girl managed to marry below her own level. The kind of man my dad would have called 'lower than a snake's belly,'" said Art. "About the only time that girl comes around is when she wants to unload her kids on Carrie. Or needs a place to stay because they've gotten kicked out of whatever dump they're living in. It's a sad situation."

"Sure sounds like it," I concurred.

Art reached into the box for the last item and unwrapped an eight-inch long figurine resembling a plump gingerbread man. The puffy little guy had only tiny round indentions for eyes and his mouth was a slightly larger O. No nose. No other features.

Art transferred the clay boy from one hand to the other, flipping him over as he changed hands. "Well," he chuckled, "it would seem that one of Carrie's grandkids tucked in his own creation without Carrie knowing it. It hasn't even been fired – just sunbaked."

Scooping a piece of paper from the box bottom, he scanned the handwritten list and nodded. "Yep, Carrie only shows three pieces on her consignment slip." Shoving the crumpled newspaper into a waist-high wire basket labeled "Packing Paper," Art assured us, "Everything's here and in perfect condition. I must have interrupted my burglar before he could take anything."

"Wait a minute," he added. "You didn't leave your figurines here, did you?"

"Nothing I make is worth breaking in to steal. And besides, they're out in the car." Millie pointed a thumb toward the alleyway. "After you left in the ambulance, we came back and Officer Stanford let me put the boxes back in Judy's car. They're still in there. I'll bring them in before we take off."

"So where are you ladies going?" Art asked as he placed my

treasures into one of his elegant black shopping bags. Gold script proclaimed "Art in the Park" diagonally across the front. Above the lettering, a single artist's brush rested atop the silver outline of a painter's palette dotted with brightly colored circles.

"Whiter Than Snow," I told him as I accepted the proffered bag. "I'm teaching the Bible study and Millie's doing arts and crafts with the children."

Whiter Than Snow had been a dream of mine, Larry's, Millie's, Bill's, and several other members of the Chalybeate Springs Community Church. Located about halfway between my home and Millie's, Chalybeate Springs has a population of around 3,500, of which as many as 300 are newcomers – legal and illegal Hispanic immigrants who have become the main residents of Chalybeate Mobile Home Park.

Unlike other mobile home communities, Chalybeate's owner was nothing more than a slum lord. Horace Brumley owned every trailer in the park and many of them dated back to the 1970s when his parents had developed the place and kept it clean, neat, and respectable. Now that Horace was at the helm, everything was in disrepair and a simple glimpse from the entrance left no doubt as to the extent of the poverty and misery within.

While there were no regulations to protect the tenants either from Brumley or each other, the rules for Horace's all-inclusive rentals contained strict limits on water and electricity usage and astronomical penalties for anyone who dared exceed these limitations. Brumley seemed to take perverse pleasure in providing washers and dryers in most units, knowing that he'd receive a pretty penny in overage fees from any newcomer who was naïve enough to use them.

Twelve years ago, Carlos and Rosa Moncada had come to Chalybeate Springs from Honduras, and both had been on staff at our church almost since the day of their arrival. Carlos directed an outreach program to the Hispanic community and was in charge of the Spanish-speaking service on Sunday mornings and Wednesday evenings. Rosa worked in the day care center, plus the couple often made extra money helping out in the kitchen during banquets or other special events.

The Moncadas' first home in Chalybeate Springs was one of Brumley's trailers, but in less than two years, they were able to buy a fixer-upper cottage within walking distance of the church. Over time, they'd turned it into a veritable dollhouse. Carlos was truly a jack-of-all-trades and could swing a hammer as easily as he could thump a Bible. Between his skills and Rosa's hard work and eye for a bargain, the two had been able to remodel, furnish, and decorate on the smallest of budgets. The plants and yard work donated by my Master Gardener friend, Gwen, put the final touches on what has already been a two-time winner of the town's Beautification Award.

Yet Carlos and Rosa couldn't forget the people still stuck in that miserable old trailer park. During one of our Bible studies,

Rosa talked about the conditions in the park and, through her concern and compassion, the vision was birthed for a free laundromat for anyone who could use that kind of help. And that's how Whiter Than Snow became a reality.

Carlos, Larry, and Bill spent months scouting out possible locations and finally selected an abandoned furniture store within a quarter mile or so of the trailer park. It'd taken a pretty serious hit during one of our recent tornadoes. The owner had taken the insurance money and run, relocating his business closer to the new shopping center and leaving the old building to crumble. Thanks to Bill's accounting smarts, the church was able to negotiate a win-win lease-purchase agreement.

Church and community members, as well as people from neighboring areas, donated washers and dryers, and a couple dozen men and women spent countless hours creating a laundromat paradise. The front of the building had been made into two large rooms with a dividing wall made of sheetrock on the lower half and Plexiglas across the upper portion. Washers and dryers filled the room on the right while the one on the left had been transformed into a children's area with kid-size tables and chairs and a play area with giant blocks, a wall-mounted TV, and shelves of books and toys.

Both rooms were painted a brilliant sky blue, but the children's room included clouds, a rainbow, and a big smiling yellow sun – all compliments of Millie and her entourage of assistants. My contribution? I spent my time shopping for and hauling in the supplies, furnishings, and equipment. As the Bargainomics Lady, I'm all about the bargains, and this project required dollar-stretching savvy out the wazoo.

Thanks to my auctioneer friend Brian, I got in on the sale of an entire warehouse of building supplies that had been gathering dust for decades. Even if we did finish up with avocado green sinks and toilets, the price was right, and when Millie and her crew finished decorating, our restrooms were doing nothing but styling.

Except for the right outer wall where dryers were wall-mounted above the washers, the washers and dryers were all at floor level, allowing for the back wall of the laundry area to also be half-glassed. A door on this wall opened into a short hallway. Directly across the hall were the restrooms, while a right turn took you to another large room behind the laundry area.

Lined with comfortable sofas and chairs, this was where we taught adult Bible studies and English classes. My sweet friend Charlotte, a retired high school Spanish teacher, rotated schedules with four other heaven-sent bilingual volunteers who led the Bible study in Spanish and the ESL (English as a Second Language) class that followed.

Behind the children's area and at the left end of the hall was our fourth finished room. It was used as a study hall and tutoring station for kids from first grade through high school. At least three volunteers manned this room so one person was able to monitor each age group: elementary, middle, and high school.

It'd taken a while to work out all the kinks, but we'd finally settled on an 8:00 a.m. to 8:00 p.m. Thursday through Saturday schedule, which prevented overworking our volunteers. With our average launderer staying between three and four hours, we scheduled one-hour back-to-back classes with volunteers working six-hour shifts each day. We tried to keep the classes to around forty-five minutes each, allowing time in between for bathroom breaks, socializing, and changing out and folding loads of laundry.

Thankfully, we had enough volunteers so that most only worked one shift a week. Dear Charlotte not only taught two different classes twice a day, but did the full twelve hours each Thursday. There's definitely a sainthood in her future.

Naturally, though, any free service was sure to be abused, which was why we posted in English and Spanish a few simple rules: (1) Anyone using the laundromat must attend the onsite Bible study; (2) anyone under 18 must be accompanied by a parent; and (3) no smoking, drugs, alcohol, or foul language. While these didn't keep the place problem-free, they at least gave us a starting point for eliminating issues.

The back of the building had been left as a storage and repair area where another crew of volunteers worked on the washers and dryers, stockpiled equipment and spare parts, and took in new donations. Word of an honest-to-goodness free laundromat spread quickly and our clientele poured in from all around, guaranteeing us a full house every time the doors were open.

❖

I grabbed the tote bag containing my notes, handouts, and Bible and used my free hand to lift out one of Millie's bags of craft supplies. Together we entered the building and greeted a dozen or so people scattered around the laundry area. A tall, slender African-American woman in her early thirties came over and hugged us both, her big hoop earrings jangling accompaniment to her armful of clattering bracelets. Shonda was one of our volunteers, and her personality was as bright as her lemon yellow t-shirt.

Exchanging hellos with several regulars and a couple of newcomers, I followed Millie through the door to the children's room, which was officially labeled the Fun Room, and left her bag of supplies on the nearest tabletop. My own classroom was already packed. I looked around and inwardly hummed, *Red and yellow, black and white, they are precious in His sight.*

Mr. and Mrs. Nguyen were seated on a sofa against the outer wall. On the opposite side of Mrs. Nguyen was Vanessa Herrera, and in the first chair along the half-glass wall, Kenny Mankiller leaned over his open Bible, a single long braid of jet black hair hanging over his left shoulder. The Nguyens had come from Vietnam to Florida and eventually to Alabama. Vanessa had never offered much about her past except to say she'd grown up in Guadalajara.

Kenny hailed from Oklahoma and had come to Alabama with his brother Oscar. Both men had found work on the Dartwells'

4,000-acre farm, but Oscar had been killed last summer when he tried to jump from an overturning tractor and was pinned underneath. The hardships and tragedies among our Whiter Than Snow family could fill a swimming pool with tears.

Sandy-haired, freckle-faced Lisa Noles sat fidgeting, her left hand rolling an imaginary cigarette between her thumb and middle finger. Lisa had recently received her one-year pin from N.A. (Narcotics Anonymous) and was still fighting a dual battle against drug and nicotine demons.

Dusky-dark Kiki Roberts rubbed her expansive belly, her swollen feet clad in pink Dollar Tree flip-flops. Kiki's baby was due any day now, and the walk from the trailer park had to have been exhausting. With two boys in the Fun Room with Millie, Kiki was looking forward to her little daughter making her appearance. And talk about a small world, we'd learned that Kiki's cousin Walter is a police officer who frequently works with Detective Metz.

I counted 23 students, marked them off my check list, and started the lesson.

Carrie Parker stared out the window above her kitchen sink and lifted up a silent prayer for endurance as she watched the ancient Toyota pickup roll to a stop by the pump house. Its battered body was now a sickly pink, but Carrie could remember when Mac had brought it home a bright cherry red. He'd been so proud of that brand new truck. Said he couldn't believe he was able to get the financing. Carrie had been sick that he'd managed. It had taken her seven long years and a heap of pots and doodads to get that thing paid for. Then Mac had gone and got himself drowned, and she'd been left with a vehicle she had no idea how to drive.

She'd been so happy when her married teenage daughter had offered to teach her. "But first, Mama," she'd said, "I need to drive it a few days and get used to it myself." The days had turned into weeks and then months and then years. For a long time, Carrie had brought it up to Jewel on occasion, but she always had her excuses. "Mama, you know Ray John's truck ain't got no tires on it. They's as slick as owl manure. And your grandbabies' daddy has got to have a way to get out and do his job huntin'."

Carrie's whole life had been one hard row after another, and one thing she'd learned: some fights just weren't worth having. She'd tasted Mac's fists more times than she could count and had seen enough bruises on both the grandkids and Ray John to know better than to get on Jewel's bad side.

That old pickup reminded Carrie a lot of herself. She'd never say so out loud, but she'd been a looker in her younger days. Light brown hair that turned almost blonde in summer, big green eyes, and long, dark lashes. And a figure to boot. Mac had called her "prettier than a princess," and her 16-year-old heart had been swept away by all his flattery and flirtation. But that was a long, long time ago, and there were few good memories of Mac after their first couple months of marriage.

The slam of the screen door interrupted Carrie's thoughts. "You ready, Mama?" Jewel mumbled around the unlit cigarette clinched in her teeth. Dumping the contents of a lime green vinyl handbag onto the counter, she made a show of rummaging through the sizable mound of clutter.

"See this?" Jewel waved a cell phone before dropping it back on the junk heap. "Useless. We got to get me some more minutes." She shoved the pile around and let loose a string of expletives followed by, "I had me a good lighter in here. I bet that stupid Ray John took it with him." Jewel huffed over to the stove, turned on one of the gas burners and leaned in, holding her hair back with one hand while sucking in the flame until the tobacco glowed red.

Carrie watched in silence, willing this time with her daughter to be over. "Where are the young'uns?" she questioned.

"I left 'em at home," Jewel responded. "And don't look at me like that! Ray Ray's not a baby no more, Mama. He's nigh on eleven. He can take care of Sissy and Nubbin."

A pang of grief washed over Carrie as she thought about how much her oldest grandson missed out on while caring for his four-year-old siblings. "How'd they take the news about their daddy?"

"Fine, I reckon," Jewel answered. "Ray Ray went out behind the trailer and snubbed for a while, but the twins didn't even look up from the television when I told 'em."

"You ain't even said nothin' about my hair, Mama," Jewel shifted topics. "After I seen me on TV, I made a appointment to get this mop fixed," she grinned. "I got a cut and color and even had 'em do my nails while they was at it." Jewel fluttered all ten blood-red nails in front of her as she squinted through the cloud of smoke curling from her lips.

"You look real nice, Jewel," Carrie told her. The last thing she needed was to say the wrong thing and set off that temper.

"Well then, we best get a move on." Jewel began sauntering toward the door. "And don't forget your credit card, Mama."

Morris Riddenbach was the third generation of his family to operate Riddenbach Mortuary. When Morris took over, he added the crematory services which Jewel Fitzhugh was now requesting. Or rather, demanding.

Jewel's white spandex capris and red low-cut tank top were not the typical wear Mr. Riddenbach saw on grieving widows. But then again, Jewel Fitzhugh didn't appear to be grieving.

"Mrs. Fitzhugh," Riddenbach began, "the coroner hasn't yet released the body." He cleared his throat and added uncomfortably, "Due to the unusual nature of your husband's demise."

"Dead's dead," Jewel snapped. "He'll be here before too long, and I just want all this mess over and done with. Short and sweet. I don't want no service, and I don't want no fancy vase or jar or whatever you call them things you put the ashes in. A cardboard box will do just fine. Mama, pay the man and let's get on outta here."

Carrie Parker dutifully presented her piece of plastic to Mr. Riddenbach and began to mentally calculate how many of her clay creations she'd have to sell to pay off Ray John's cremation.

Art had never been so thankful to hear his clock's five sturdy bongs that signaled closing time. Even though several friends had stopped by and offered to drive him home, Art had opted to walk, a decision he now realized had been a bit premature. By the time he'd made it the two blocks between his house and business, his entire body was screaming for relief.

Grabbing a bottle of water from the fridge and downing two of the pain pills the ER doc had prescribed, Art collapsed onto the sofa and clicked on the television. The evening news was already in progress.

"Still no arrest has been made concerning the murder of Raymond John Fitzhugh whose body was found near the Glaze Creek landfill in Veramosa Thursday evening. Although few details have been released at this time, an anonymous source within the police department says that Fitzhugh had likely been killed elsewhere earlier that day and his body then left at the Glaze Creek location."

"Oh, poor Carrie," Art mumbled as he drifted into medicated slumber.

13

When Jewel Fitzhugh pulled up in front of her trailer, she muttered a few choice words as she noted the door standing open. Slamming the truck door, she flicked her spent cigarette into the weed-spotted dirt and stomped over to the single cinder block that served as a step. Wailing sirens could be heard coming from the television and she could see Ray Ray in one of the recliners and the twins crammed into the other.

"Dad-blame it, Ray Ray!" she yelled above the blaring TV. "What have I told you about leavin' this door open? We're gonna be eat up with bugs in here, boy! What's the matter with you?" She punctuated her rant by crossing the room and smacking the side of her eldest son's head before snatching the remote and jabbing the "off" button.

"It's hot, Mama," Ray Ray answered matter-of-factly as he rubbed the side of his head. "And the fan quit workin'."

"Well, ain't that just great," Jewel fumed. "At least they ain't done cut the power off."

Sissy pulled a dirt-ringed thumb out of her mouth and swiped at a mass of golden brown ringlets. "That man called," she said.

"What man called what?" Jewel questioned her daughter.

"Tell her, Ray Ray." Sissy looked to her big brother for assistance.

"We heard a phone ringing and found this down in the recliner," Ray Ray said, holding out the phone by way of explanation. "Some man said to tell you he wanted his merchandise. He talked funny."

So that sneakin' dog had his own cell phone, Jewel realized. Snatching the phone from Ray Ray's hand, she bellowed, "Think, Ray Ray! What else did he say?"

"I don't remember," Ray Ray insisted, throwing one arm up between himself and his mother.

Fearing another lick was about to come her big brother's way, Sissy interjected, "But he wroted his number, Mama. It's right there on the table."

In three strides Jewel was at the rickety dinette. Three mismatched plastic bowls and an empty Cheerios box were scattered across the cracked Formica surface. An assortment of flies and smaller insects vied for the bowls' dredges while a single yellow jacket drank from a streak of clabbered milk that striped the table. Jewel spied the scrap of paper with Ray Ray's crayon-scrawled numbers.

Instinctively, Jewel drew a fingernail to her mouth, then remembered her manicure and thought otherwise. "You kids go on

64

outside and play," she ordered. "I got business to tend to."

Easing nervously into Sissy and Nubbin's vacated recliner, she placed the call and felt her heart hammering as she waited for the connection. "Mrs. Fitzhugh," The Collector intoned in a raspy growl. "I heard about your husband's tragic passing. My sympathy to you and your children."

"Uh, thank you," Jewel responded.

"And now it seems I have somewhat of a problem, Mrs. Fitzhugh. Jewel, isn't it? For the sake of expedience, would it be acceptable for me to call you Jewel?"

"Yeah, I guess so," Jewel answered, clueless as to his four-syllable word's meaning.

"Raymond was in possession of a piece of merchandise he'd agreed to sell me, Jewel. And it's very important that we are able to complete that transaction. Do you understand me?"

"I thought that's what Ray John did last night, Mister, uh… I don't believe you told me your name."

"I did not, nor will I give you my name, Jewel. But let me clarify our situation, shall I? Raymond made two very foolish mistakes last night. One, he came to me empty-handed. Two, he had the audacity to suggest a higher price than what we'd agreed upon. These two things, I should stress, precipitated his untimely demise."

Jewel frantically tried to assemble her thoughts. *This ain't the kind of person you play games with. Ray John mighta been dumb enough to try for more money, but he woulda never showed up without it unless he never got it back.* Now she was very sure she knew where to find what he wanted.

"Are you tellin' me Ray John tried to hold you up for more money?"

"Indeed," The Collector answered. "He made me very, very unhappy. I expect you, Jewel, to change that."

"Well, see," Jewel began, "I don't exactly have it with me. But I can get it," she rushed to explain.

"Then do so. Are you aware of where Raymond was instructed to meet me?"

"Sure, the old ..." Jewel started. But The Collector immediately interrupted.

"A simple 'yes' will suffice, Jewel. Be there at one a.m. And not empty-handed."

"Ten thousand dollars is a lot of money, Mister. How do I know I can trust you?"

"Trust me, Jewel?" The Collector blew out an exasperated breath. "It would seem that your husband was the one who could not be trusted. The figure was one hundred thousand."

Jewel sat bolt upright and clamped her free hand over her mouth lest she shriek into the telephone. Jewel Parker Fitzhugh was going to be stinking, filthy rich. She'd been willing to take a chance for ten thousand. But ten times that? She'd swim a piranha-infested river for that kind of money.

"I'll be there. I swear. And I'll bring it with me." She fought down the tremor that threatened to overtake her whole body.

Jimmy studied The Collector's face as the call ended. "Boss, I don't get it," he said. "She thought she was gettin' ten grand and you went and told her you'd pay a hundred?"

The man's heavy-lidded eyes turned to his associate. "One hundred thousand dollars is an inconceivable fortune to a woman like Jewel Fitzhugh. Her entire focus is now on the prize, not the danger." A malevolent smile lifted the corners of his pale, thin lips. "Once Mrs. Fitzhugh and I become better acquainted, I believe she will refuse any payment. I will indeed obtain a remarkable bargain. One might even say, a bargain to die for."

"Ray Ray!" Jewel bellowed from the doorway. "Get your brother and sister and get in here. We're going to your granny's."

Jewel handed the kids off to her mother and whined, "I'm gettin' one of my sick headaches. Y'all don't make no racket. I'm goin' to bed." She turned into the first bedroom, closed the door, and locked it.

Carrie looked at her trio of grandchildren and sighed. "It's nigh on nine o'clock, and I bet ya'll ain't had a bite to eat. Y'all hungry?" Three heads nodded enthusiastically. "Ray Ray, run take a quick shower while I put some supper together." Turning to the grimy twins, she smiled weakly. "Nubbin, pull a chair over to the sink, and let's get you and Sissy cleaned up some. Y'all can take your baths in a little bit."

Jewel raised the window at the side of the bed so she could blow her cigarette smoke outside. She was in no mood to deal with her kids or her mother. And she was tired. Bone tired. If she laid down, she'd fall asleep for sure, and she couldn't afford that.

It seemed like an eternity, but was probably no more than a couple of hours, until the house grew quiet and Jewel was certain everyone was in bed. Silently removing the screen and pulling it into the bedroom, Jewel slipped out the window and scurried around the side of the house.

She congratulated herself for thinking ahead and parking the truck away from the house. Softly closing the truck door, she switched on the ignition and pushed in the clutch. Instantly alert to the muffled crunching of her tires as the Toyota rolled toward the roadway, she scanned the house for any sign that someone had awakened. She saw nothing. Engaging second gear, Jewel eased out on the clutch, lightly touched the accelerator, and the engine leapt to life.

14

Jewel had shoplifted, pickpocketed, and panhandled. She'd even accompanied Ray John on a couple of B&Es, but she'd never broken into anyplace singlehandedly. She parked the truck several blocks from her destination, pulling Ray John's dark blue coveralls over her ensemble and topping it off with a black hooded sweatshirt. Drawing a tire iron from under the seat and shoving a flashlight into the pouch of her hoodie, she began her walk down the alleyway.

Traffic noises drifted up from Twentieth Street and a few dogs barked in the distance. But as she passed the dumpster in back of Delhi Delight, a black blur darted in front of her, frightening her enough that she let out a yelp that echoed off the tightly-packed buildings. "It's just a black cat," she whispered. "Good thing I ain't superstitious."

She crossed the three side streets and finally arrived at the back of Art in the Park. Faint fingertips of moonlight brushed the doorway as Jewel pulled out her tire iron and began to pry against the door jamb. The groan of the metal frame was instantly followed by an ear-piercing alarm. Stumbling backward, Jewel dropped the tire iron and took off running.

Jewel pulled to the farthest reaches of the truck stop's sprawling blacktop. Shucking off the coveralls and tossing them onto the seat atop her sweatshirt, she leaned her forehead on the steering wheel and fought back tears of frustration. Minutes passed before she sat up, switched on the dome light, and adjusted the rearview mirror to check her reflection.

"Ray John sucked a lotta life outta you, girl, but you've still got your looks. And that's what I call negotiatin' power." She dug a lipstick and a loose breath mint from the bottom of her purse, popped in the mint, and coated her lips with a layer of Red-iculous Crimson.

Jewel stifled a giggle as the chauffeur held open the door of the sleek, black limousine. Never in her life had she sat in one. Scooting across the luxurious leather upholstery, she gazed over at The Collector and couldn't help thinking of the statues of that fat smiling Chinese guy that were sold at the Mini-Mart. Except The Collector most definitely wasn't smiling. Nor was his musclebound companion.

"Disappointment, Jimmy," The Collector spoke to his driver

through the open partition. "Yet another disappointment we must deal with."

"But, sugar," Jewel told him, drawing out the last word as she leaned in and tickled her fingernails along The Collector's doughy mitt, "I can show you exactly where to find it. I can show you more than that," she added provocatively.

Quick as a striking cobra, The Collector engulfed her hand in his, squeezing even harder as she cried out in pain. "You pathetic, fatuous gutter snipe," he intoned, punctuating each word with bone-crushing pressure. "Do you think I could find your advances anything other than repulsive?" He released his grip and Jewel drew herself up, shaking in terror as she shrunk away from him.

"I can get it. Just give me one more chance. I won't let you down," she pleaded.

"There are no more chances for you, Jewel. I simply need you to tell me where it is. And then our business will be concluded."

"You mean, you'll pay me if I tell you where to find it?" Jewel spoke quietly, her racing heart slamming against her chest.

"No, Jewel, that's not what I have in mind," the man answered.

"What are you going to do?" Jewel hardly recognized her own tremulous voice.

"Do, Jewel? Whatever would give you the idea that I would bother doing anything to you?" He slowly smiled as he saw the relief wash over her features.

"That, my dear, is Jimmy's department. And I can assure you, he really gets into his work, don't you, Jimmy?" Jimmy turned and his profile revealed a malignant grin.

"Please," Jewel begged, now quaking uncontrollably. "I've got three kids that need me. And you need me to show you ..."

"I hardly think so, Jewel," The Collector interrupted unemotionally. "It would seem you're as much a failure as a thief as you are a mother. Jimmy," he ordered, and Jimmy quickly appeared at the open back door of the limo.

"You've heard the expression, 'cut up the middle man,' haven't you, Jewel? Or is that 'cut out'?" A sulfurous laugh belched from his throat. "My little play on words," he continued. "And, I'm afraid, a present reality for you, Jewel."

The Collector exited the car and strode untroubled along the riverbank as Jewel Fitzhugh's screams pierced the still, inky darkness.

This had been so unnecessary, Jimmy thought, as he observed the ball of flames that had been Jewel's pickup. The young junkie he'd hired to drive the truck to this remote location had been well compensated for his services and then had the audacity to demand more money.

It was the principle of the thing, Jimmy mused. Not that he'd planned to let him live in the first place. But he'd had a painless demise planned for his hireling, which had changed when he'd had to teach him a lesson. If you crossed Jimmy Sarnecki, you'd suffer the consequences. And suffer he had.

The kid was supposed to help him push the truck into the water, but when he'd made his threat, Jimmy had decided to go a different route. He always had a backup plan. He put the gas can back into the trunk of the little white Hyundai and drove away, the orange glow lighting the night sky behind him. He had one more stop to make before daylight.

15

Saturday morning temperatures were already in the high eighties as Larry and I loaded into the Fit and started our one-hour drive to Smith Lake. We'd bought an older motor home from Larry's aunt and uncle and had put a lot of TLC into making it roadworthy before deciding to park it at Harvey's Marina for the summer. So far, we were enjoying being RV-ers, and hoped to take a serious road trip sometime in the fall.

Smith Lake, or more correctly, Lewis Smith Lake, is a manmade reservoir stretching over parts of Walker, Winston, and Cullman Counties. With more than 500 miles of shoreline, Smith offers some of the finest fishing around and is especially popular with fishers of striped and largemouth bass.

Weekdays, when half the population of Alabama wasn't out on the water, were ideal times to pack a lunch, hop on our Sea-Doos, and enjoy a day of exploring. But not today. Watercrafts were as thick as swarms of bees, so our only plan was to stop by long enough for Larry to change out the leaky kitchen faucet while I threw together a simple picnic lunch.

En route to and from, we had one goal: to bargain shop. Which is exactly what we were about to do. Larry spotted the first yard sale sign and we pulled to the roadside, joining a half dozen cars and pickups. A large brick rancher had a driveway filled with tables and racks of possible treasures. Bright blue tarps were spread over the lawn and covered with a smorgasbord of household goods, books, toys, shoes, and tools. I knew where Larry was going.

I've been the "Bargainomics Lady" for years now. I started out writing articles about how to stretch a dollar, and that soon expanded into writing regular columns, doing speaking engagements, getting my own radio show and, later, weekly and semi-monthly TV segments. Today I'd hoped to find a few things we could use in the motor home and a new jacket or outfit to wear on television.

I was in luck. The first table had a nice two-slice toaster for only a dollar. I scooped it up and kept searching. On one of the clothes racks, I hit real pay dirt: a burnt orange designer label jacket that was a perfect fit and tagged at only $10.

Larry appeared at my side, holding a cigar box filled with an assortment of drill bits. "Two dollars," he said, a hint of a smile telling me he'd landed a serious bargain.

Larry has been the love of my life since early high school. As a lowly sophomore, I'd been rushing down the steps to make it to English class when my face slammed into a purple number 55 football jersey stretched across a most impressive chest. I'd looked

75

up into a tanned face with eyes so brown I couldn't see the pupils. His jet black hair was a short-cropped mass of unruly curls, but it was his eyes that had held my attention. More than thirty years later, they still do. In this girl's slightly biased opinion, Larry Bates is the sweetest, cutest guy on the planet.

By the time we pulled up by the motor home, it was only a few minutes shy of high noon and we'd already shopped three yard sales, a thrift store, and a discount grocery. We each snagged a bag of groceries from the back of the Fit and took them inside to add to our meagerly stocked kitchen.

Sunday. "How'd the bargain hunting go?" Millie asked as she slipped into the choir loft beside me. "I had a booth at the Art Walk and since *vous* were not available to help me, Bill had to give up his big gardening day to be my assistant."

"OK, I owe you one," I admitted. "We did great. You're gonna love the Windsor china teacup and saucer I got. I talked them down to twelve dollars."

"Impressive," Millie returned. "But here's what I really wanted to ask you. Have you talked to Art this weekend?"

"No, is there some reason I should have?"

"Guess not, but he called me this morning to let me know he sold two of my little angels and that watercolor of Cheney's Mill. He also told me," she lowered her voice, "that the guy whose body was found in Veramosa Thursday evening was Carrie Parker's son-in-law."

"Oh, how awful," I responded.

"And that's not all." Millie leaned in even closer. "Somebody tried to break into Art in the Park Friday night."

"What…" I began, but just then Leslie, our music minister, moved into position and the orchestra began the opening hymn. "You're still helping me tomorrow, aren't you?" I hurriedly whispered as Leslie motioned us to stand, then quickly touched a finger to her lips, warning all of us to end our conversations.

"I'll be at your house at 10:30," Millie answered, "but as you've already pointed out, you owe me. Big-time."

This is where my reference to Vanna White comes in. As often as possible, Millie accompanies me to my speaking engagements. I don't merely talk Bargainomics. I bring along a lot of show 'n' tell items and Millie walks around the audience and shows them off. In exchange, I'm her assistant at art shows whenever I can.

Today I was presenting Bargainomics at a corporate brunch, which, in this case, meant a mile-long conference table full of men and women. In this setting, my show 'n tells could be passed around the table, so the biggest reason for Vanna coming along was because I owed her lunch, and it was her turn to choose the location.

Introductions over, I lifted an object from the podium and held it aloft. "What," I asked, "do you call this?"

"A hammer," a chorus of voices responded.

"And a hammer is?" I questioned this time.

"A tool," came the answer from all around the table.

"Now let's suppose I take this hammer, place it in the hands of a two-year-old, and leave her in this room alone for one hour." Snickers from all around the table. "Know what we'd get? It's called *destruction*." Another round of laughter.

"But," I continued, still holding up the hammer, "let's say I put this same hammer into the hands of a carpenter and leave him alone for one hour. I, ladies and gentlemen, would end up with the exact opposite result. It's called *CONstruction*. Same tool. Completely opposing results."

I had their interest, but the point was still a mystery. "What made the difference?" I asked. "Simple. The skill of the operator."

And now the light bulbs were glowing. "Money is a tool. It requires an operator. Therefore, it will never work any better for you than you know how to use it."

I took a spin around the room, modeling and describing my newly purchased jacket and the rest of my outfit. Returning to the podium, I hit the highlights of a dozen or so ways to cut expenses.

16

"So tell me about this break-in," I urged Millie as we loaded all my show 'n' tells back into the Honda.

"Art said his new alarm system saved the day," Millie told me. "Whoever it was dropped a tire iron they were apparently using to try to pry the door open. The police have it and are hoping to get some fingerprints."

"A burglary and an attempted burglary in less than a week?" I mused. "Did Art say if any of the other stores had reported any problems?"

"That's just it," Millie answered. "His is the only shop that's been bothered."

"Then it would seem the thief's quarry is still in the building," I suggested.

"That's the only thing that makes sense," Millie concurred, slamming the hatch and scooting into the front passenger seat.

"I think it's time to go back to Art's and do some real digging. And this time we won't leave there 'til we figure out what this burglar is after."

"Let's do it," Millie agreed. "But first, feed me. And secondly, swing by the post office so I can buy some stamps."

I heard my wallet groan when Millie announced her choice of Dupree's for lunch. At least, I consoled myself, I had a coupon for a 20 percent discount. Seated outside near the fountain, we salivated over our menus as we made our decisions.

"Excuse me," a voice spoke from the tableside. "Aren't you the Bargainomics Lady?" She eyed me expectantly.

"I am," I responded, smiling brightly and standing. "And this is my cousin, Millie Caffee." Millie nodded and went back to her menu.

"I told you it was her!" the woman called to her companions. "We watch you all the time," she gushed. "Love the deals you tell us about. See this purse?" She held it out for my inspection. "It's a Coach. And I got it at Three Sisters, that consignment shop you mentioned several weeks ago."

By now the rest of her entourage had us surrounded. "Forty-five dollars," the woman added, patting her handbag. "And Darla, tell her about your jewelry."

Darla was wearing an exquisite turquoise necklace that, she informed me, had come from King's Home Thrift Store for only ten dollars. Valerie had visited King's Home with Darla and had landed her Kate Spade sundress for fifteen dollars. The rest of the group all had similar bargains and all credited me for their fabulous fashion finds.

"I am totally impressed," I told them. And I meant it. Nothing got me pumped like seeing other ladies – and men – showing off their bargain hunting finds. "Thrift store" was no longer a word to be whispered. My fans and I loved shouting it from the rooftop.

As soon as my impromptu fan club meeting broke up, Millie put her menu down and snorted. "May I touch your hand, Miss Judy? Get your autograph, please?"

"Knock it off," I told her. "You're just jealous."

"You know I'm just messin' with you," Millie replied. "But it never ceases to amaze me how often people recognize you. I mean, do you remember that group in Washington, D.C. who started waving and running toward us? How can somebody with five minutes of local fame a week get so much attention?"

"Well, in case you've forgotten, I do write books, too. And articles, and regular columns, most of which include my photo. And there's also my website, Facebook, and Twitter. Plus I've been on a couple of national TV and radio shows."

"Okay, I get the picture," Millie interrupted.

"I think, though, the biggest reason people like me is because I'm the real deal. No fluff. No pretense. Just practical money and time-saving ideas. There are too many 'bargain'" – I held up my fingers as quotations marks – "gurus who want to tell you how to save $100 on an $800 outfit. Or how to make your own placemats with $40-a-yard fabric. People appreciate me because I live in the

81

real world and pass along information they can really use."

That said, we discussed our food options and made our decision. I closed my menu and one very patient waiter stepped forward.

"We'd like to share a salad and entrée," I told him. "We'll have the portabella salad and the shrimp and andouille fettuccine. And we'd like them brought out at the same time, please."

Like everything served at Dupree's, the salad was a work of art. Roasted portabella mushrooms nested on a bed of fresh mixed greens generously sprinkled with goat cheese, toasted sunflower seeds, and Dupree's own honey Dijon dressing. Our entrée was loaded with sautéed shrimp and andouille sausage in a creamy Alfredo sauce over fettuccine that our waiter generously topped with freshly grated Romano cheese. Life was good.

And getting better. Sharing the entrée meant room for dessert, so we ordered a slice of their incredible sweet potato pecan pie and two cups of Café du Monde coffee and chicory.

If you're not familiar with Café du Monde, this New Orleans hot spot's original location in the French Market has been in business since 1862 and their beignets (the square, fried, powdered sugar-dusted Cajun version of a doughnut) and Louisiana style coffee have gotten so popular that they've expanded into several locations and have begun selling their beignet mix and fabulous coffee in-store and online. Dupree's was one of a number of upscale restaurants that now offered their coffee.

After finishing off the last crumbs of our pie, Millie and I spent another fifteen minutes relaxing and enjoying our coffee before heading back to the car. Minutes later, we were at the post office where Millie disappeared inside for what seemed an eternity. While I was waiting, I remembered the folk planters in the back of the car and made the decision to go in and mail them. My Norwegian friends Per and Iren adored flowers and pottery, so these would be the perfect gift for their 25th anniversary.

My task completed, I met Millie on the way out, a shopping bag draped over her arm. "Really?" I asked, arching one eyebrow. "You've been shopping in the post office?"

"It so happens that Bill and I are doing stamp collections for all our grandkids," Millie answered.

"Sounds thrilling," I deadpanned.

"Shows how much you know," she responded. "Stamp collecting is one of the most popular hobbies in the world. When Bill and I were in Hartford, Connecticut last year, we went to a big stamp show put on by the American Philatelic Society, and it was really fascinating."

"Well, excuse me for not feeling giddy over my Forever stamps," I told her.

Carrie had wanted to keep the kids quiet Saturday morning, so she'd sent the younger two outside where they were less likely to wake their mother. When Ray Ray went to check on them, he ran into the kitchen, banging the screen door behind him and causing Carrie to cringe in dread of Jewel's reaction.

"Truck's gone," Ray Ray announced. "Ain't no tellin' where Mama went off to."

"Oh, mercy," Carrie muttered, walking to the bedroom door and trying the doorknob. "It's locked. Ray Ray, go outside and see if you can climb in through the window."

Moments later, Carrie heard the lock turn. The bedroom door opened and Ray Ray pointed at the bed by the window.

"See, Granny, it ain't even been slept in. Shoot, Mama probably skedaddled out that window as soon as she went in there."

And Ray Ray was probably right, Carrie knew. Jewel had always been a sneaky one.

Now here it was midday on Monday and they hadn't heard hide nor hair, which, even for Jewel, was unusual. The grandkids seemed oblivious to their mother's absence, thrilled to be where it was safe and quiet and they knew they'd be well fed.

Deep in thought, Carrie mechanically ladled up bowls of venison stew and placed a plate of piping hot cornbread in the center of the table. Adding a glass of lemonade to each setting, she checked to make sure the Heinz was by the salt and pepper – those young'uns could sure go through the ketchup.

The screen door scraped and creaked as Carrie stuck her head out and called, "Y'all come wash up. Lunch is ready."

Inside Art in the Park, Millie and I changed into jeans, t-shirts, and sneakers and began, with approval from Art, examining every nook and cranny behind the showroom. Dividing the area into sectors, we meticulously moved every object from whopping crates to mounds of cleaning rags. Not one item turned up that Art wasn't able to identify.

"I'm telling you, ladies, I'm at a total loss to figure this out. A burglary and then an attempted burglary with nothing missing or even damaged – except for my noggin." Touching the back of his head, he winced in discomfort.

"Then there's only one thing we can conclude," I said, still looking around in utter bewilderment. "Whatever the thief was after had to be small enough to cram in a pocket."

"That doesn't make a lick of sense!" Millie protested. "If he'd gotten away with whatever he was after, why would he come back and try to break in a second time? Duh!" She rolled her eyes at my hopeless stupidity.

"Right," I admitted. "It's just so baffling."

"That it is," Art agreed.

"So what now?" Millie asked.

"I'm out of ideas," I confessed. "At least the new alarm system should prevent any further break-ins. In the meantime, I'll drive you home and then have a talk with one of my favorite policemen."

My daddy, Ellis Woodward, is a blueblood. No, he isn't royalty – except in my eyes – but he had carried a badge for 30 years and has investigative skills that would shame any bloodhound. (Millie would probably disagree on account of Jethro Bodine, but that animal doesn't even know he's a dog.)

Daddy lives in a retirement village called Lost Gap, the residents of which sardonically refer to it as "Last Gasp." Running from all the community's widow ladies keeps him fit as a fiddle.

"I don't know where to put anything else," he'd told me only a couple of weeks after moving into his ground-level apartment. He'd opened his fridge and freezer and displayed a stockpile of casseroles and cakes that could last him for ages. "Welcome gifts,"

Daddy chuckled. "And," he added with a wink, "I've taken a pass on offers of a lot more than cooking." That was when I assured him I didn't need further details.

I'm undoubtedly a bit biased, but on the hunk scale, my dad's a ten and a half. With a headful of thick silver hair, blue-gray eyes, and not an ounce of fat on his five-ten frame, he's the envy of every male Last Gasper and the heartthrob of all the ladies. Somehow he shrugs it all off and tries to be equally friendly with everyone.

My beautiful mama went to heaven five years ago. Daddy stayed in their house for three more years but finally decided he wanted a smaller space with less upkeep. At Last Gasp, he has a nice two-bedroom apartment with a screened porch in back and a tiny raised garden.

Like many other residents, Daddy still drives. However, at the time of the move, he had sold his four-year-old Buick and stunned Larry by giving him his one-owner '66 Chevy pickup.

He kept one car, his pride-and-joy '56 Chevy Bel Air, now hidden beneath a custom-fitted cover and nestled in Daddy's designated parking space. The immaculate red and cream two-door sported an automatic transmission, air conditioning, power steering, and every other modern gadget Larry had been able to install without compromising its classic appearance.

❖

When Daddy and I rolled up at Dairy Queen, every head turned to admire the Chevy. Parking in the farthest corner away from the other vehicles, we made our way inside and ordered our favorite Blizzards: a Turtle pecan cluster for me and a Chocolate Xtreme for Daddy.

By the time, as Daddy put it, "our fannies hit the chairs," a man came over to our table. "Here it comes," Daddy said, casually looking up from his spoonful of ice cream.

"I saw y'all get out of that '56 over there," the man began. "Beautiful car. Would you be interested in selling it?"

As usual, I sat there with a goofy-looking grin, barely restraining a gut-wrenching belly laugh. How many times we'd been through this scenario, I couldn't begin to count. But I knew what was coming; I'd heard Daddy say it a jillion times.

"You don't see a 'for sale' sign on it, do you?" Daddy asked, eyes twinkling with merriment.

"No. No, sir, I don't," the man acknowledged.

"That's because it's not for sale," came Daddy's coup de grace.

"Well, if you ever change your mind …" The man drew out his wallet and extracted a business card.

Daddy waved it away. "Son," he said, "my daughter here has already claimed that car, but I hope she has to wait a few more years to get it."

The man smiled, shook Daddy's hand, and went out the door, casting one more admiring look at the Chevy before driving away.

We both burst out laughing, drawing more than a few looks from other Dairy Queen patrons.

"You get entirely too much pleasure out of doing that," I told him.

"Well, people ought to quit asking if they don't want to hear it," he responded. Truth was, Daddy would've been heartbroken if he didn't get to pull that stunt at least once every time he took the car out.

"Now," he said, dipping up another huge glop of chocolaty goodness, "tell me about this break-in."

"In this day and time, it could be something as tiny as a pinhead," Daddy pointed out. "Microchips. Microdots. Jewels. Coins. So many really small objects can be worth a lot of money and easy to stash."

"I don't know," I countered. "Whoever broke into Art's can't exactly be the brightest bulb in the box, or he wouldn't have had to make a second attempt."

"That's not necessarily true," returned Daddy, "since Art did walk in and interrupt him. But the fact that he botched the second try shows he didn't know much about reconnaissance. Otherwise, he'd have been aware of the new alarm system and been prepared to disarm it."

"So where do we start from here?" I pondered.

"Well, I've got a buddy, Vince Forsythe, with a TSCM service who could do a sweep of Art's place and see if anything turns up."

"A what?" I queried.

"A technical surveillance countermeasure service," Daddy explained. "They look for electronic bugs and such."

"So if the thief was after some kind of electronic thingy, he could find it. Is that it?" I asked.

"That's it," Daddy answered. "Want me to give him a call? He owes me a favor."

At 45, Carrie Parker felt 90. She hadn't wanted to call the police, but after three days, what else was she to do? She'd sent the kids outside while she talked to the deputy. He'd made out his report, but Carrie knew any search would be minimal.

She also realized she'd have to find a way to get over to the trailer park and get more clothes for the children. And she knew her strength was not going to get her through this trouble.

After a quick peek out the door to make sure the kids were okay, she went into her bedroom and lifted her well-worn Bible from the nightstand. Seated on the edge of the bed, she began to read Psalm 121, making every word a heartfelt prayer for herself, Ray Ray, Nubbin, and Sissy. "I will lift mine eyes unto the hills, from whence cometh my help. My help cometh from the Lord ..."

"Did, too!"

"Did not!"

The twins charged into the kitchen, Ray Ray trailing behind them. "Y'all better cut it out," he warned them. "Granny! Sissy and Nubbin are fightin' again!"

Carrie stood, closed the Bible, and moved slowly toward the kitchen.

Daddy had left the military and become a cop shortly after he and Mama were married. By the time I came along, Daddy had worked his way up from beat cop to detective and, later, I suspect, had done some stints working undercover. What else could explain his months-long absences?

Once I remember waiting in the car while Mama ran into a post office on the other side of town. She'd said she was going in to mail a letter, but I saw her opening a mailbox and taking out a letter that she kissed and hugged against her before tucking it into her handbag.

Daddy's never talked about his time in the military, either, but I think he must have been some sort of Special Forces or something. Once, when I was a kid, he and I were coming out of Loveman's Department Store in downtown Birmingham when a man called out to him.

"Sergeant!" the man shouted, hurrying toward us. "Never thought I'd lay eyes on you again."

We stopped and Daddy studied the man's face. "I'm sorry. I can't seem to place you."

The man did a quick salute. "PFC Nathaniel Murphy, sir," he said. "You may not remember me, but I sure remember you, Sergeant."

Looking at me, Mr. Murphy asked, "Is this your daughter?"

"Yes, this is Judy," Daddy told him. Then turning to me, he

added, "This gentleman and I were in the service together."

"That's all you've got to say, sir?" Mr. Murphy looked surprised. "Why, your dad saved my life. When he and his men busted into that prison in …"

"That'll do, Murphy," Daddy interrupted. "Sugar, why don't you stand by the door and wait for your mother while Mr. Murphy and I talk a few minutes."

When Mama came out onto the sidewalk, I pointed at Daddy and Mr. Murphy and said, "That man said Daddy saved his life. Is that true, Mama?"

I still recall the pride in her eyes as she looked at my father and answered, "He saved a lot of lives during the war, honey, but he doesn't like to talk about it."

And that was as close as I ever came to knowing anything about what my daddy did in Vietnam.

Before walking him to his door, I'd helped Daddy put the cover back on his Chevy. Now I was ready for home, a glass of iced tea, and my recliner. As I headed to my car, Right Said Fred's "I'm Too Sexy" sounded from my cell phone. Larry calling.

"Hi, hon." My husband's voice sounded chipper. "How'd your speaking engagement go, and what else have you been up to?"

"Good," I said in answer to the first part of his question. "And to lunch at Dupree's and then to Art's …"

"Did you find anything?" Larry interrupted.

"No, but Daddy knows a guy who …"

"Let me guess," Larry chuckled. "Owes him a favor?"

"Yep," I answered, laughing, too. "He's going to do some kind of sweep for electronic doohickeys to see if there's some kind of microchip or something the burglar might have been trying to find. I'll tell you the rest when I get home and can get some supper started."

"That's why I'm calling," Larry explained. "Bill and I are meeting at Whiter Than Snow so we can help unload some of the new donations. We'll grab something to eat when we finish up there."

"All right, then," I told him. "After the lunch I had today, a salad will be enough supper for me. I'll see you when you get home. Love you bunches." I didn't bother to mention the Blizzard I'd had a little later.

"Right back at ya'," he responded.

An hour later, I was up to my chin in bubble bath, my salad bowl and tea glass balanced on my bath tray, and a classical music station on my TV where Andrea Bocelli was beautifully serenading me with *Con Te Partirò*. On the vanity, my cell phone began to do a little dance as the opening strands of Paul Petersen's "My Dad" interrupted my concert. Lunging across the bath tray, I snatched up the phone.

"Hey, Daddy. Is everything okay?" My father didn't make too many unimportant phone calls.

"Wanted to let you know Vince will be at Art's tomorrow. 0900." That's 9:00 a.m. to us civilians.

"I assume Art's okayed this," I questioned, knowing full well Daddy had every base covered.

"He has," Daddy answered. "We both," (meaning he and Art, I presumed) "thought you might want to be there."

"I'd really like to," I told him sincerely. "But I've got to go to WEEE to record some promos for my segment."

"Understood," said Daddy. "You know," he added, chuckling, "the Last Gasp folks think my daughter is some kind of celebrity."

"Well, I am," I declared. "For five minutes a week, anyway. How'd you talk Vince into helping us out?" I asked, knowing full well the answer.

"He owed me a favor," Daddy answered.

If I had a nickel for every time I'd heard my daddy speak those words, I'd be rolling in money. Daddy seemed to "know a guy" for every situation.

"Well, let me know if y'all find anything," I told him. "Matter of fact, call me whether you find anything or not."

By the time I'd dried off, dressed, and carried my plate and glass into the kitchen, my phone was serenading me again, this time with strands of *"Ja, vi elsker dette landet,"* the national anthem of Norway. I wondered which Norwegian friend I'd find on the other end of the line.

"Hello?" I hit the speaker button and set the phone on the countertop.

"Judy," a deep male voice spoke. "How are you, my dear?"

It was Per (pronounced like *pear*) Nordstrand, calling from Norway. Per is one of the Norwegian friends I mentioned earlier. He, along with his entire family, had become friends and then more like family to me and Larry. Years ago, Larry had gone with me on a writing assignment to cover the National Quartet Convention in Louisville, Kentucky. We met Per and his brothers when I'd interviewed them after they'd been introduced as the number one Southern Gospel group in Norway.

"We are definitely number one," Per had told me in perfect English. "Because we're the only Southern Gospel group in Norway."

After that first divinely appointed meeting, we'd stayed in touch and, a couple of years later, had the opportunity to see them again while I was covering the Gospel Music Convention in Fraserburgh, Scotland. We all ended up staying an extra week and traveling together to see more of Scotland and to become better acquainted. Per's wife Iren and I instantly bonded and still find so many similarities between Larry and Per that we suspect they were somehow separated at birth.

Since that first meeting, we've regularly taken turns visiting each other, plus meeting to vacation together in different locations. We've watched their children grow up and marry and seen their grandkids come along. We've fallen in love with their country and with the rest of the Nordstrand brothers and their families, and gotten to know a lot of other folks on Huftarøy, their island home just off the coast of Bergen.

"Doing great," I responded. "So how's crime in Kolbeinsvik?" Per is the Chief of Police (called a *lensmann*) for the municipality or *kommune* (not a city, but comparable to what we'd consider a county), of Austevoll, which includes the town of Kolbeinsvik on Huftarøy.

"We haven't had a crime wave, but I did have to handle an interesting situation a few days ago," he told me. "An old man who lives on a farm far out on the end of the island came in and reported that one of his sheep had been stolen."

"We don't get a lot of sheep thieves around here," I told him.

"Well, this was the third time this man had reported something missing from his property," Per explained. "So I started thinking."

When Per says "I started thinking," he means he's onto something. Whether it's his years of experience as a policeman or his sensitivity to the needs of others – or maybe a combination of both – he's very, very good at his job.

"So what'd you do?" I questioned.

"I went out to his farm and had a look around while he wasn't home. I found the sheep tied in his boathouse. I also found the other two items he'd told me were missing."

"Was the man going senile or something?" I offered.

"No, I think he was very lonely. I didn't want to embarrass him, so I brought the sheep up to the house and waited for him to come home. When he got there, I told him I had found it, but didn't mention where and didn't mention the other items. Then I suggested that he make us some coffee so we could sit and talk a while. When I left, I told him I'd start coming by every week for a visit and that maybe that would keep the thief from coming back anymore. He agreed that would probably take care of the problem."

I loved Per's stories about the island, and I loved how he handled the situations. Sure, there were more serious crimes from time to time, but it was his Mayberry-like stories I enjoyed hearing.

"And I bet it does," I laughed. "But you didn't call to tell me about a sheep thief. What's up?"

"Iren is in Spain with some of her girlfriends, and she wanted me to find out if you and Larry had made your travel plans yet." Iren's brother Ian (pronounced *Yon*) has a condo on the beach in the south of Spain and lets the family use it whenever it isn't rented. For Norwegians, hopping over to Spain is like Alabamians flying over to Texas. It just sounds a lot more glamorous.

"I'm planning on booking everything this Sunday," I told him. "And when Iren gets home from her trip, we're going to nail down our travel plans for when we get to Norway."

"Nail down?" Per queried. "Does that mean making the plans firm?"

"Exactly," I told him. Per was really getting good at figuring out our expressions and colloquialisms. "So now that we've talked all this time, was there a specific reason for your call?"

"Actually," Per sounded a tad apologetic, "I meant to call Larry's mobile, but called yours instead."

We both laughed, and I explained that Larry was probably having supper with Bill by now. "How about I get Larry to call you tomorrow?" Looking at the clock on the oven, I realized it was going on 2:00 a.m. in Norway. Per kept some really weird hours.

"Sounds good," Per responded.

"It was nice talking to you even if you didn't mean to call me," I teased.

Tuesday. My phone began playing "My Dad" as I drove through the gate leaving the station. "What'd y'all find?" I questioned.

"Nada," Daddy responded. "Vince didn't find a thing. Whatever the thief's after is definitely not electronic, but it's undoubtedly still in that building. You want to have another go over the stockroom?"

"Between Art, Millie, and me, I don't think we left a stone unturned, but if you're volunteering to take another crack at it, I'm in," I told him. "But I can't do it today. How about first thing in the morning? I've got a couple of articles to finish and I need to get them emailed by in the morning."

"Tomorrow, 0600, then?"

Daddy's and my idea of "first thing" weren't exactly the same. "Uh, I was thinking more like 0900, Daddy. I'll be fully conscious by then and I'll even make you breakfast if you want to drive out here and us ride together."

The gallery's phone rang as Art walked a customer to the door and thanked him for his substantial purchase. Carrie Parker was on the line.

"Hi, Carrie," Art answered. "How are you?"

"I ain't so good, Art. Jewel left the young'uns with me and took off sometime Friday night or early Saturday morning, and I ain't seen or heard from her since. I know she's a wild one, but she ain't never done me like this."

"Is there anything I can do to help?" Art asked.

"That's why I'm callin'. I hate like the dickens to ask, but I was hopin' you could come get me and pick up some of my clay pieces. Ray Ray, Sissy, and Nubbin ain't even got a change of clothes over here, and I ain't got no dryer. I been washin', but they have to wear Mac's old t-shirts around until their clothes dry. It ain't so bad for the lit'l 'uns, but Ray Ray's big enough that it embarrasses the fire outta him."

"I can understand that," Art responded, "but I know you're doing the best you can."

"I am," Carrie replied matter-of-factly. "But that's the mainest reason I'm askin' you to come. I wanted you to carry me to the trailer park and let me get some of their clothes and see if maybe Jewel's there. I tried callin', but then I remembered she don't have no more minutes on her phone right now. I've done called everybody else I can think of, and I ain't been able to get a-holt of a soul. I'm 'bout ready to set off walkin' if that's what it takes."

"No need for that," said Art. "I'll be by there as soon as I close up the shop. But I don't have any car seats for Sissy and Nubbin and I'm not really comfortable with driving them around without them."

"I understand," returned Carrie, "but I ain't plannin' on takin' the young'uns along. As bad as I hate puttin' 'em off on Ray Ray, he's used to watchin' after them lit'l 'uns, and I don't rightly know what we'll find at the trailer park. Best they not be there."

"A wise decision," Art agreed. "I'll see you this evening."

I got home in time to put a nice late lunch together: grilled chicken salads smothered in homemade bleu cheese dressing and topped with croutons and extra crumbles of bleu cheese. Larry had been out all morning mowing our property. Besides an acre and a half of landscaped lawn, we have another four and a half acres of field and forest, along with a small pond we'd stocked with bass, bream, minnows, and grass carp. At only a half-acre, it wasn't much compared to our neighbor's six-acre lake, but we enjoyed it.

I prepared the salads, put them on a tray, and carried them down to the tiny cabin we'd built by the pond. Placing the tray in the seat of one of the porch rockers, I unlocked the cabin and selected two glasses from a small wall-mounted cabinet. Collecting napkins and utensils as well, I extracted the ice tray from the mini-fridge and plopped cubes into both glasses before bringing them out to the porch. After adding these items to the tray, I rang the big cast iron bell that was mounted by the porch steps. On the opposite side of the pond, Larry waved from the tractor. There's no way he'd heard the bell above the noise of the tractor running, but he'd spotted me and started maneuvering in my direction.

After washing up inside the cabin, Larry dropped into one of the rockers and I placed the salad-laden tray in his lap. I'd brought another tray out of the cabin and stocked it with my share of the lunch goodies. We munched in appreciative silence, watching our resident kingfisher alternately perched in a waterfront cowcumber magnolia or dive-bombing a zigzagging school of minnows.

Our one-hundred-twenty-foot-square cabin had been inspired by my friend Gwen. She'd helped me design it, and Larry, jack-of-all-trades, and I built it and furnished it on a very meager budget, using a whole lot of thrift store and yard sale bargains. It had become my writing retreat where I could hide out uninterrupted and pound the keyboard for hours. On other occasions, Larry used it as his nap spot after a long morning of yard work. Speaking of which, I figured he'd be working on that nap as soon as he'd finished his salad.

"I meant to stop in time to watch your segment, but I let the time slip by me," my overall-clad Prince Charming told me. "Is that what you wore?" he asked, referring to the sapphire blue tank and matching burnout jacket I was wearing.

"It is," I responded, "but I was recording promos. Nothing was live or aired today. And I was hungry and didn't even bother to change when I came in. Figured you hadn't stopped for lunch, either."

"And you figured right," he responded, setting his tray on the porch floor and leaning down to plant a kiss on my forehead. "How about after my nap, we catch some fish and I'll fry them up for supper?"

"Sounds like a plan. How about I join you for that nap?" I suggested.

And that's exactly what we did. An hour later, I walked up to the house and changed into jeans and a t-shirt, slathered on some sunscreen and my favorite sunhat and met Larry on the pier. In less than an hour, we'd caught our supper. A few hours later, we were chowing down on fried fish, slaw, baked potatoes, and hushpuppies. Gotta love a man who can cook like that.

Larry and I heaved ourselves from the table, determined to go ahead and clean the kitchen before sitting down in front of the television. We finished in time for the nine o'clock news and snuggled into our reclining loveseat to see what was happening.

A weeping elderly woman was being interviewed by a reporter. "It's not right," she was saying, shaking her head and wiping her eyes with a tissue. "He only paid me twenty dollars."

"This was the scene in Hulett, Wyoming this morning when

collector Cyril Pennylegion announced he was auctioning a newly discovered Anna Moses painting for an opening bid of one hundred thousand dollars," Janet Hill announced, looking squarely into the camera.

"A small framed farm scene by the artist better known as Grandma Moses was among the items being sold in this woman's yard sale. She says she had no idea the 'Moses' scrawled in the corner was anyone famous."

"How come when I buy a painting for twenty dollars, it turns out to be worth fifty cents?" I griped. "Can we skip the news tonight? I'd like to watch something where the good guys win for a change."

Larry agreed and began scanning the program guide. We decided on "Road to Morocco" with Bob Hope and Bing Crosby. Sometime later, I awoke to find Larry gently snoring beside me and an infomercial onscreen telling me how I could lose weight without ever exercising or dieting. If only. I shook Larry awake and we trundled off to bed.

Art had carefully loaded a dozen plastic Walmart bags, each containing a Carrie Parker creation, into the back floorboard of his battered Subaru wagon. Hitting the Red Mountain Expressway, Art was relieved to have missed the worst of the evening traffic.

"I'm real sorry about not havin' my stuff boxed up for you, Art," Carrie began. "But I reckon them young'uns has been out in my workshed and tore up ever' box I had out there."

"No problem at all," Art assured her. "I've got plenty in the storeroom and we'll load you up when we leave."

Pulling up against the back of the building, Art hopped out and went around to open Carrie's door, but she was already halfway out of the vehicle. "Ain't used to no gentleman," Carrie smiled.

Disarming the alarm and opening the back door, Art stepped in and flipped on the bank of switches for the overhead lighting. Carrie brought in the first load and, within minutes, she and Art had emptied the Outback and placed all the bags on the storeroom counter. After putting together an unwieldy stack of cardboard boxes, Art had Carrie unlock his car, then assist with filling the cargo space with the boxes. Turning back to the shop door, he secured the lock, reset the alarm, then reclaimed his place in the driver's seat. Next stop: Chalybeate Mobile Home Park.

Art was thankful to note that it wasn't quite 7:30, which hopefully meant getting in and out of the trailer park before dark. The place had a reputation, and while some of the residents were just poor folks trying to get by, others were dangerous, scary people who Art prayed they wouldn't have to deal with.

The old pickup was nowhere in sight as Art snugged the Subaru as close to the trailer as he dared and then asked Carrie to wait. "Give me a minute to poke around," he said. "Then I'll come get you." Reluctantly, Carrie obeyed.

Stepping up on the cinderblock, Art tried the knob. "It's unlocked," he called. What he didn't say was the door had been pried open. The edge of the metal door was bent outward and around the lock, the door jamb was smashed into splinters. "Hang on a sec."

Peering through the doorway, Art saw that even the Fitzhughs couldn't have made the mess he was seeing. Their shabby furniture had been gutted. Tables, lamps, and chairs were overturned, and dishes were broken and scattered. Cheap framed prints had been ripped from the walls and torn from their frames. Art pulled out his cell phone, walked to the open doorway, and held up one hand to signal Carrie to remain in the car.

Reaching into his wallet, he extracted the card Detective Metz had given him during his own fiasco and dialed the cell number the policeman had handwritten on the back. He answered on the second ring.

"Metz here. Who's calling?"

"Detective Metz, this is Art Molina from Art in the Park. I'm out at Chalybeate Mobile Home Park in the trailer belonging to Ray John and Jewel Fitzhugh, and…"

Metz interrupted with, "What the blue blazes are you doing there?"

"Well, the short version is I have Jewel's mother with me and I brought her out here to get some clothes for Jewel's kids."

Metz interrupted again. "Where're the kids? Where's Mrs. Fitzhugh? And what are you doing with her mother?"

107

"Listen, I'll explain everything, but right now I need you to send someone over here. This place looks like it's been in a hurricane. The kids are at Carrie's and they're fine, but their mom has gone missing."

"I'm on my way," Metz said. "Don't touch anything. Get out of the trailer and wait in the car." Art heard a beep and the detective was gone.

20

By the time his unmarked car screeched to a halt behind Art's Subaru, Metz was out of the vehicle, hand inside his jacket where, Art suspected, Metz was reaching for the weapon in his shoulder holster. The officer nodded at the duo in Art's car and signaled for them to stay put. Minutes later, he stood in the trailer door and motioned them inside.

"Somebody's torn this place apart," Metz announced unnecessarily. "Had to be looking for something." Turning to Carrie, he asked, "Ma'am, I'm really sorry about your son-in-law, and I mean no disrespect, but do you know if he or your daughter were involved with anything illegal? Drugs? Gambling? Anything like that? I have to ask."

"I understand," Carrie assured him. "And I don't know what to tell you. My daughter didn't marry well, Detective. Ray John was out of work more than workin'. If they was into anything illegal, they must not've been very good at it because they was always broke and hittin' me up for money."

Tears trickled down Carrie's cheeks and Art patted her shoulder as her voice trembled. "Be that as it may, Jewel's still my daughter, and I don't want no harm to come to her. She ain't been the best daughter or mother, but not once has she gone off like this without so much as a note or a phone call. I'm scared, Detective. I don't believe she'd run off and forget her young'uns like this."

It was nearly ten o'clock by the time Detective Metz finished questioning them and confirming that a missing person report had been filed on Jewel. As soon as Carrie had rummaged through the debris and found enough clothing to fill a pillowcase, they were on their way. At Carrie's, every light in the house was on as the car rolled up the driveway. He wore a brave face for a ten-year-old, Art thought, but he could still see the relief as Ray Ray opened the door for his grandma.

Art pointed his car toward Carrie's workshed, parked, and lifted out the stack of boxes. He used his headlights to illuminate the narrow path through the field of knee-high weeds, then shoved open the unlocked door with the toe of his sneaker. Placing the boxes on the floor, he pushed them back enough to close the door.

It must have been 80 degrees by the time the sun came up Wednesday morning. We were in for a scorcher. Having years of previous experience with dear ol' Dad, I was dressed, ready, and mixing up a batch of pecan pancakes by 0730 when Larry, who was on the screened porch downing his first morning cup of coffee, stuck his head through the doorway.

"Your dad's here."

"And breakfast'll be ready in a few minutes." I'd already fried some bacon and sausage and had it warming in the toaster oven. "Pour him a cup of coffee and tell him to park it at the table."

I'd already set the table, so now I only had to carry out a tray. I stacked it with pancakes, sausage, bacon, a bottle of maple syrup, and a small pitcher of melted butter. Transferring the vase of wildflowers from the tabletop to the tray, I placed the tray and all its glory in the center of the table and took a seat between my two favorite men in the universe.

"Daddy, you want to ask the blessing?"

The black limo was far too noticeable, so after they'd dealt with the Fitzhugh problems, The Collector had handed Jimmy a roll of cash and instructed him to "obtain an inconspicuous vehicle" from Rent-A-Heap or another used car rental company. He'd already given him a Mississippi drivers' license in the name of James Compton. Compton, Jimmy had chuckled, looked amazingly like Jimmy Sarnecki.

He'd also decided nothing could be less noticeable than his

mom's old Hyundai, so he'd opted to forgo the rental and hang onto the money. He did, however, leave a couple of twenties on the kitchen table after wrenching the car keys from the old bat's bony clutches.

Not that he'd needed keys, of course, but bending a few fingers was less work than hotwiring. And besides, he deserved a bonus for the work this job was turning out to be.

What had started out as a simple transaction had become far too complicated and required keeping an eye on more people than he could keep up with. If only he and the boss could hire someone to help out from time to time. But Jimmy knew that would never happen. When it came to their temporary help, they'd always relied on the process of elimination. One and done. No witnesses, no worries.

As the copper-colored Honda motored along Twentieth Street, Jimmy trailed behind a couple of car lengths. Suddenly the Honda driver whipped into the outer lane and made a right turn. Jimmy cursed and followed as horns blared and brakes screeched all around him.

"Make a right!" Daddy ordered. "We've picked up a tail." Obediently, I sped up and changed lanes, barely squeezing in front of one very unhappy driver.

"Why would anyone be following us?" I asked after I made

the turn onto the side street. "Are you sure?"

"Positive," Daddy answered, eyeing the side mirror. "Keep your eyes straight ahead," he commanded as I glanced toward the rearview mirror. "A white Hyundai Accent has been tailing us since we came through Gardendale. And he's still less than half a block behind us."

"So what do we do now?" I wasn't exactly trained for evasive maneuvers.

"Speed up and duck into that alley," Daddy ordered as we neared Cobb Lane.

I shot into the alley, tires bouncing and rumbling on the ancient brick paving. "He's hitting his brakes!" I shrieked. "He knows where we went! Now what do we do?"

"Stop and change seats with me. Quick!" Daddy's voice was firm but calm. I obeyed and, within seconds, he had us turned around and nosed to the front of the alleyway. As the Hyundai whipped in, Daddy floored the Fit and zipped past it, barely avoiding a head-on collision. The swerving Hyundai slammed into the brick wall, and we made our escape.

I was shaking from head to toe, but Daddy was driving as if being chased by crazy people was an everyday occurrence. Of course, in his years on the job, he'd probably had plenty of practice. But not me. Had I not also been in danger, I think he'd have been enjoying the whole adventure.

"Did you get the license number?" Daddy asked, pulling back onto Twentieth.

113

"You aren't serious, are you?" I looked at him incredulously. "I was a little preoccupied with survival, and it never even crossed my mind, to be honest."

"My bad," he said apologetically. "I should have told you to beforehand. Guess I'm a little rusty at barking out orders."

"Oh, I think you're still as bossy as ever," I teased as my nerves began to settle.

We drove around Southside for at least an hour, pulling off here and there and keeping an eye out for a banged-up white Hyundai Accent. When we were sure we were no longer being followed, Daddy drove straight for Art in the Park but opted to park at a meter some distance away. We hoofed the few blocks to the gallery and tapped on the front door.

"Hi, guys," Art greeted us as he unlocked and let us inside.

"You won't believe what we've been through," I told him, and then gave the full account of what had happened.

"This is getting absolutely crazy!" Art declared. "We've got to get to the bottom of this before someone else gets hurt."

"Or killed," Daddy added, looking worried. "All these things are connected," he said, and began ticking off the events on his fingers. "Ray John Fitzhugh's murder; Carrie Parker's pottery; your assault; and probably even Jewel Fitzhugh's disappearance. Am I leaving anything out?"

"Art had another attempted break-in," I added.

"Y'all are probably still pretty shaken from the car chase. Let's have a glass of tea and sit for a few minutes before we get started. I don't open for another half-hour," Art reminded us. "And if it's too early for tea, I can make y'all some coffee."

Summer in Alabama? Uh-uh. It was never too early for a glass of iced tea.

A few minutes later, we'd pulled three folding chairs into a circle in the middle of the storeroom floor and were sipping our tea and mulling over the past few days' occurrences. I, for one, needed the time to get my heart out of my throat after our wild ride through Southside, but Daddy seemed to have taken the whole thing in stride.

"This may not even be worth mentioning," Art began, "but Carrie said something about the boxes in her workshed. But first, let me back up and fill you in on yesterday evening." Art then related his trip to Carrie's and their visit to Jewel's trailer.

"Wow! It seems we've all had more than our share of excitement," I declared.

"We don't know how many people are involved in this, but I think it's safe to assume it's not one man working alone," Daddy stated. "And the torn-up trailer could mean one of three things: either Jewel ran off with whatever our mystery man, or men, is after; she's run off in fear for her life because these people believe she has whatever they're looking for and she really doesn't have it; or she's been killed by these people because she refused or was unable to cough up whatever they're after."

"What if they're holding her hostage?" I suggested.

"If that were the case, Carrie or someone would've gotten a

115

phone call by now," Daddy pointed out.

"And as not-so-nice a person as Jewel seems to be, I don't think she'd run off and leave her kids without at least letting her mother know she was okay," I added to our theories. "Carrie herself said that much to Art."

"True," Art agreed. "Besides, Jewel has never been able to manage much on her own. If she were in trouble and able to make a phone call, Carrie would have heard from her. If she had money or something of value, I really believe she'd have either taken her kids with her or come back for them. No, I think it's down to the worst-case scenario. More than likely …"

We all finished the sentence together: "… she's dead."

On that cheery note, we began our umpteenth search of the storeroom, this time with the help and savvy of Daddy. After a few minutes, Art had to go out front and open up, but he came back to help until the doorbell signaled the appearance of a customer. Art returned as often as possible to help with our quest.

By noon, we'd run out of places to check or recheck and we'd found absolutely nothing. Finally, Daddy turned to Art and said, "I want you to close your eyes and visualize this storeroom just as it was before the original break-in. Forget about anything that's come in since that time and focus only on what should be here from last Thursday."

Art sat motionless for several minutes, then opened his eyes. "I'm sorry, y'all, but other than the folk art planters Judy bought that day, nothing's been moved out of the storeroom. Except for a stack of cardboard boxes I gave to Carrie."

Daddy rubbed his chin and stared at the floor before speaking. "Okay, so if the item's not here, it has to be in one of those two places: the planters or the boxes. Judy, where'd you put those planters?"

"They're on their way to Norway. I sent them to Per and Iren as a present."

As soon as Daddy's car disappeared down the driveway, I called Larry's cell phone. Today was another garage day, but I knew he and Terrell would knock off early since it was a church night.

"Hey, my sweetie," Larry answered. "How'd the search go?"

"Me, Art, and Daddy took the storeroom apart again and didn't find anything. Not only that, Art took Carrie over to the trailer park to get clothes for the kids, and the trailer had been totally trashed. I know you're busy, so I'll explain more when I see you, but I was wondering if it'd be okay if I met you at church this evening?"

"I guess so," Larry responded, "but aren't you at home by now?"

"Yes, but I'm leaving again," I told him. "I'm meeting Daddy, Art, and Detective Metz out at Carrie Parker's."

"Isn't that out of Metz's jurisdiction?" Larry questioned.

"Yes," I replied, "but he said it was worth checking since the missing mystery item might be there and it was a probable link to Art's assault and break-in."

"Say no more," Larry assured me. "I'll see you at church. And," he added, "be careful."

"We will," I promised. "I love you."

My next call was to Norway. Per's home phone rang repeatedly. Nobody there. I tried his work number next. He'd warned me that it was super expensive to receive overseas calls on his cell, so I'd try that only as a last resort.

"Kolbeinsvik politistsjon. Politibetjent Bjelland snakker," the voice on the other end of the line told me. ("Kolbeinsvik police station. Police Inspector Bjelland speaking.")

"Hallo," I responded, "dette er Judy Bates ringer fra Alabama in USA. Jeg vil gjerne snakke med Lensmann Nordstrand, takk." (Hello, this is Judy Bates calling from Alabama in the USA. I'd like to speak with Lensmann Nordstrand, please.)

There was a momentary pause and then a male voice I immediately recognized said, "Hallo, dette er Lensmann Nordstrand." ("Hello, this is Lensmann Nordstrand.")

"Per, it's me, Judy. I'm so glad you answered because I was about to run out of Norwegian." I was only halfway joking. "I know you're busy, so I'll condense this as much as possible..."

I hit the highlights of what had been going on, concluding with, "And there's a possibility that whatever these people are looking for could be hidden inside the gift I sent for your and Iren's anniversary."

"Really!" Per exclaimed. "That is most interesting. When did you send this package?"

"Monday," I said. "So it'll probably be early next week by the time it gets there."

"I'll examine it very carefully as soon as it arrives," he assured me.

"And in the meantime, if we find it at Carrie Parker's, I'll text you and let you know what it is," I promised.

By the time I got to Carrie's, Daddy and Art were already there. Carrie and the three of us stood outside the workshed, waiting for Detective Metz as we'd been instructed. Ray Ray, Sissy, and Nubbin hovered nearby, their curiosity piqued by this gathering of strangers.

"You young'uns go back in the house," Carrie nervously scolded the children. As Ray Ray obediently herded his siblings away, Carrie ran a hand through her hair and heaved a sigh. "Sakes alive, a part of me wants to be mad enough at Jewel to shake her silly, but another part of me is scared to death of what mighta happened."

"We're all praying for her, Carrie," I told her.

"I know y'all are," she acknowledged, "and so am I. But bad choices can lead to bad trouble, and a way long time ago Jewel turned her back on the Lord and everything she was taught as a young'un. Can't no good ever come from that kind of livin'."

None of us could think of anything to say in response, so it was a relief to see Detective Metz's car coming up the driveway. He parked near the other three vehicles and began walking toward us.

"I'd know that '56 Chevy anywhere," were Metz's first words. "Woody, it's really good to see you." He grinned at my dad and stuck out a hand.

"Good to see you, too, Metz," Daddy returned.

What Detective Metz couldn't have known was that no one inside or close to the family called Daddy "Woody." At a family reunion, if you called out that name, you'd have every male Woodward's attention. Seems as though all the guys' coworkers or schoolmates stuck them with that label.

"So you and my dad know each other?" I queried.

"Your dad?" Metz lifted an eyebrow. "Why, Woody, you never told me your daughter was a TV star."

Turning to me, he added, "You look a little different without all the twigs in your hair."

"What?" Daddy asked.

"Never mind. I'll explain later," I told him. "In the meantime, back to my question. How is it you two know each other?"

"I worked my very first case alongside ol' Woody," Metz told me. "It was a joint task force operation, and your dad was heading it up for the state. Hey, Woody, remember those two hookers we busted…"

"That's enough history, Metz," Daddy stopped him. "Let's get to the business at hand here."

Carrie's workshed was exactly that – a shed she worked in. No bigger than my and Larry's tiny cabin, it was unpainted and slightly leaning. The ancient wood walls were grayish-black and the rickety old door was equally weather-beaten. The dark metal doorplate was rusted and pitted, but the doorknob itself was smooth from the countless times Carrie had turned it. Metz stepped inside and lifted the ungainly stack of boxes from the floor as Carrie flipped on the lights. The rest of us entered behind them.

"Mrs. Parker, if you'll clear us a spot along this table, please," Metz requested, indicating a long section of planks nailed to the left wall opposite Carrie's potting wheel.

Carrie moved a half dozen items to the far end of the table and Metz began placing individual boxes along the open space. "Each one of us will take one box," Metz instructed. "Go over every crevice and, if no one finds anything, then we'll begin taking the boxes apart. And in case we turn up anything, better wear these," he added, pulling a wad of latex gloves from his jacket pocket. "The boxes have already been handled repeatedly, but there could be viable prints on the inside."

There were seven boxes and only five of us, but seven people would never have squeezed into such a tight space. As it was, we were wedged in like high noon at a lunch counter. We worked in silence for several minutes, inspecting and re-inspecting every inch of our boxes, but found nothing.

"Let's start taking them apart," Metz instructed. "Just go slow and easy. And stop if you see or feel anything that doesn't seem to belong or if you have a question."

My box had an office supply store label and had once been filled with printer paper. I gingerly pried one side loose and then another, until I finally had the box laid out as a flat piece of cardboard. As I began separating the overlapping pieces inside the bottom section, I caught sight of a tiny sliver of white paper.

"Detective!" I called. "Come take a look at this."

Metz studied the bit of white for a few seconds, then produced a pair of tweezers and began cautiously tugging it from beneath the overlap. I was too short to see over Metz's shoulder, but when he held it up still clamped in the tweezers, I could see it was an inch or so square with something printed on it.

"What does it say?" I demanded excitedly. Everyone had pushed in around us.

"Inspected by number 22," Metz announced. We all laughed half-heartedly. We'd so hoped we'd found the mystery item.

When Metz went back to his own box, I went back to pulling the bottom of mine apart. When I had finished, I'd found no more inspection notices or anything else.

Suddenly Carrie let out a soft gasp. "Detective, I may have somethin' here," she almost whispered.

Once again, Metz took over as we all huddled around him. Cardboard, or corrugated boxes, are made in three layers. An inner layer of paper is folded into furrows and ridges and then glued between two smooth sheets of paper, creating a fairly sturdy container for storage and transport. With Carrie's box, someone had pried part of the center section loose, enabling them to slide a small flat object inside it. As Metz's tweezer once again did their job, we held our collective breaths and waited.

Once it was free from the cardboard, Metz laid the tweezers on the table. "It's wrapped in what looks like regular ol' kitchen plastic wrap," Metz said. Carefully peeling back the plastic, he revealed what appeared to be a very old photograph. A young man wore his hair parted in the middle, reminding me somewhat of an older version of Alfalfa from The Little Rascals. His shirt was emblazoned with the word "Pittsburg" and underneath the photo was printed "Wagner, Pittsburg."

All three of the guys had apparently been struck speechless, but Carrie hadn't seemed to notice. "That's just one of Grampa's old baseball cards," Carrie told us. "Why in the world would anybody go to so much trouble to hide somethin' like that?"

"Blame it all," she fumed. "It had to be Ray John that done it. Ray Ray was here last Wednesday. Why, that was the same night you come picked up my clay pieces, Art," Carrie recalled. "Anyhow, Ray Ray was over here and I'd told his mama she either had to bring him some church clothes or come git him 'cause he was as nasty as a pot. She said she'd send his daddy after 'im.

"Before he got here, though, I come out here to wrap the pieces that was ready to sell and box 'em up for you, Art. Well, while I was out here, Ray Ray had got into a ol' cigar box I keep in the top of my closet – that boy will get into anything that ain't padlocked. Anyhow," she continued, "he pulled that card out and

124

was settin' at the kitchen table with it in his hand when I come in from the workshed. I told 'im them keepsakes was special to me and not to be meddlin' in 'em.

"With all that's gone on, I clean forgot I never did put it back up. Don't even remember seein' it after that. I'll bet you a nickel Ray John stole it off the table when he come got Ray Ray. But why?" Carrie questioned. "And why would he hide it like that? It just don't make no sense."

"Mrs. Parker," Metz said when he regained the power of speech, "let's go in your house and sit down and talk about this."

We trooped into the kitchen and were immediately joined by the three grandchildren. "Ray Ray, go put your brother and sister in the tub and help 'em get ready for church," Carrie ordered.

"But, Granny," Ray Ray protested. "I wanna hear what's goin' on."

"You'll hear soon enough, boy," Carrie told him. "Now skedaddle."

"Yes, ma'am," came the reluctant reply. Ray Ray trudged off, herding Sissy and Nubbin ahead of him.

When we were all seated around the long wooden trestle table, Metz reached over and gently held Carrie's hand. "Mrs. Parker," he began, "I don't know any way to prepare you for what I'm about to say, so here goes. The reason your son-in-law went to so much trouble to hide this baseball card is because it's worth a whole lot of money."

At that, Carrie said, "I can't believe that. What kinda money are you talkin'?"

"Well," Metz answered, clearing his throat and barely restraining his excitement, "this particular card sold at auction a few years ago for just under three million dollars."

Stunned silence. While Art and Daddy had seemed somewhat prepared to hear this astronomical figure, I was, appropriately for the situation, out in left field with Carrie.

"Say that again?" Carrie's voice quivered.

"Just under three million dollars," Metz repeated.

"But," Daddy rushed to add, "the factors that determine the value are things only an expert could really tell you."

Art could contain himself no longer. "At the very worst," he interjected, "it's probably worth in the neighborhood of five hundred thousand."

Carrie placed both elbows on the table and buried her face in her hands, sobbing uncontrollably. I stood and walked around to stand behind her, my hands on her shoulders.

"I know this is a lot to take in ..." I began.

After a long, awkward moment, Carrie looked up, steepled her hands, and breathed, "Jesus, Jesus."

"This is a real blessing, that's for sure," I told her.

"True enough," Carrie agreed. "But this," she indicated the baseball card now lying in the center of the table, "may've not only cost Ray John his life, but Jewel's, too. If she knowed they was money to be made, there ain't no tellin'," she whispered, glancing around to make sure the children were still out of earshot.

"It does look like this card may be what started this whole chain of events," Detective Metz acknowledged. "I'm betting Ray John saw a program about baseball card collectors that was on the History Channel a few weeks ago, because that's why I recognized the card when I saw it."

"But like Carrie said earlier, why not just take the card instead of hiding it like that?" I questioned.

"I'm merely guessing," replied Detective Metz, "but if his wife saw the same program he saw, it could be he wanted to keep his find a secret from her, too."

"Now that makes sense," Carrie said, nodding her head and picking up the baseball card. If this thing is worth all that kind of money, I believe I need to put it in a Ziploc bag where it'll be better protected." She rose to carry out her objective.

"Actually, Mrs. Parker …" Metz began.

"How about you dispense with the 'Mrs. Parker' and call me 'Carrie'," she suggested.

"I can do that." Metz smiled and continued. "I'd like to take the card with me, if you don't mind. We'll check it for fingerprints and see if we can figure out who else is involved in all this. And it might give us a clue as to who killed your son-in-law. I'll write you a receipt for it, and I promise to take very good care of it."

"Well, I reckon that'd be okay," Carrie told him.

Larry was getting out of his truck as I pulled into the church parking lot. Finding an open space close by, I parked, hopped out, and hurried to fill him in on what we'd discovered.

"What player was on the card?" Larry asked.

"Somebody Wagner," I answered. "He had 'Pittsburg'" without the 'h' on his jersey."

He let out a low whistle. "Honey, that could possibly be the most valuable baseball card in history. What a blessing for Carrie!"

"Yep," I agreed. "I'm really happy for her. But she's still, of course, so worried about Jewel."

With that, we walked into church. Millie spotted us as we entered and waved us into a seat beside her and Bill. "Have y'all had supper?" she asked, as soon as we were seated.

"No," I replied. "We drove separately because I came straight here from Carrie Parker's, and Larry barely got home from the garage in time to take a shower."

"We haven't eaten, either," she said. "So why don't we grab a bite to eat after the service? I've gotten all your texts about what's been happening, but if we can sit down face-to-face, you can give me more details."

"Sounds good to me," I told her. Just then, the service began and we had to end our conversation.

We agreed to meet at Lupita's, a Tex-Mex café owned by one of the many people Carlos and Rosa Moncada had helped get a start in our community. We gorged on fajitas and green corn tortillas and then ordered coffee and sopaipillas.

Larry couldn't wait to tell Bill about the baseball card and the two began an animated discussion. Millie and I merely listened and learned.

"Yeah," Larry was saying, "if it's really a 1909 Honus Wagner trading card, it could be worth a sizable fortune."

"Detective Metz said one sold a few years ago for almost three million dollars," I interjected.

"And there've been a couple more sold recently, each for more than a million dollars apiece," Bill added. "Of course, the value of Mrs. Parker's card will depend on its condition."

"What's the big deal about this Honus Wagner guy?" Millie asked.

"It's not so much the guy exactly," Larry explained. "It's the card itself. There were trading cards known as 'tobacco cards' that came with packs of cigarettes made by the American Tobacco Company. The company printed them without Wagner's consent and he didn't want his image on something that might encourage kids to smoke, so he threatened a lawsuit and forced the company not to use them."

Bill picked up the story. "So only about 200 were made before he put a stop to it. The cards were never sold with the cigarettes, but they somehow got into people's hands rather than being destroyed, as was supposed to happen."

"So they're really rare," Millie said. "I hope Carrie's is in better condition than any other one ever found."

"Well, I don't know the first thing about antique trading cards," I said, "but it looked to be in great shape to me."

We began a lively speculation on what we would do if we suddenly found ourselves with a million dollars or more to play around with. That led us to talking about buying all new washers and dryers for Whiter Than Snow, and that led us back to reality as Larry and Bill discussed the number of washers and dryers they needed to work on.

While our husbands were deep into their repair plans, I filled Millie in on the last couple days' events, starting with Art and Carrie at the trailer park; then me and Daddy being followed by the white car; searching Art's workroom again; and, finally, going to Carrie's and finding the Honus Wagner card. Millie shook her head in amazement.

"It's like a dream, isn't it?" she said. "I mean, you hear on the news about things like this happening, but you never think you'll actually know someone it happens to."

"True," I agreed. "And I'm sure Carrie's super thankful, but it's hard to get too excited when she's so worried about Jewel."

"Is there anything I can do to help?" Millie asked.

I told her about Metz's plan to check the trading card for fingerprints. "But in the meantime, if we could find any sort of clue that might help lead the police to whoever Ray John was involved with, that might put them one step closer to finding Ray John's killer and figuring out where Jewel is or what's happened to her."

"How about we go through their trailer?" Millie suggested.

"It's worth a shot," I agreed. "Could we do it tomorrow?"

"Sure," she said. "You know my shop's only 'open by chance or appointment'," she said, making quotation marks with her fingers as she cited her studio sign. "But what about your TV segment?"

"I did the morning show last week, so I'm just doing the noon news tomorrow. Let's meet at the trailer park at 9:00 in the morning," I proposed. "That should give us plenty of time to look around before I have to head to the station. Besides, we sure can't do it Friday since we'll both be teaching classes at Whiter Than Snow."

"How about, instead," Millie countered, "we meet at the church and leave one car there so we can ride the rest of the way together?"

Thursday morning. At the end of the driveway I stopped at our mailbox and stuck a card in the box, lifting the flag so our mail lady would know she had a pickup. Before I pulled away, my cell phone rang.

"Hello," I spoke into the phone.

"Judy, this is Clarice." Clarice is one of the handful of neighbors we have along our little country road.

"Oh, hi, Clarice," I responded. "How are you?"

"Fine," she returned and hurried on. "I was wondering if you know anybody that drives a little white car with a smashed front fender on the passenger side."

A knot formed in the pit of my stomach. "Not that I can think of," I answered, recalling my and Daddy's near miss with the white Hyundai Accent. I was being truthful. After all, I had no idea who the driver was. "Why do you ask?"

"One drove up and down our road several times yesterday right before church time. Real slow, like he was looking for something. When I walked outside and made it obvious I was watching him, he drove away. I'd never seen that car around here before."

No stranger drove down our street without being noticed, and I am so thankful for Clarice and the rest of our very observant neighborhood watchers. But there was no need to worry them, I decided.

"Well, if you see it again, try to get the tag number," I suggested. "And if I see it, I'll be sure and let you know." I hoped I'd never lay eyes on that Hyundai again.

I spent my drive to the church looking for the white Hyundai but, thankfully, never spotted it. Millie was already there when I arrived, so I hopped out, locked my car, and climbed into hers.

"You look a little rattled this morning," she observed. "Anything you want to talk about?"

"Oh, nothing," I said. "Just that same crazy guy who chased me and Daddy through town has apparently been nosing around my neighborhood. That's why I'd rather leave my car here and go in yours."

Millie gasped. "Have you told the police?"

"No, I didn't know about it until Clarice called me a few minutes ago."

"Well, you need to call Detective Metz," Millie insisted.

"I will," I assured her, "but let's search the trailer first, okay?"

I didn't want to worry Millie, but during the short drive over to Chalybeate, I kept up a vigilant watch for that little white car. When we parked in front of the Fitzhughs' trailer, I'd seen no sign of it. The trailer door was closed but unlocked, and the place still looked like a disaster area – so much so that even the shadier characters in the mobile home park hadn't bothered looking for anything salvageable.

"What a dump!" Millie exclaimed unnecessarily. "Where in the world do we start?"

The living room and kitchen were one room crammed with a mismatched table and chairs, and two recliners, all of which had been demolished. Stuffing lay in scattered chunks; cabinets stood open and mostly empty, their previous contents shattered and tossed in every direction.

"Right here's as good a place as any," I said. "Let's divide the room into sections and comb one area at a time."

"It'd help to know what we're looking for," said my partner-in-grime.

"A business card. Anything with a name on it besides the Fitzhughs'. Another million-dollar baseball card would be nice, too," I added.

Wearing the latex gloves we'd brought for the occasion, we dug through mounds of trash from furniture innards to things we couldn't quite identify. When a rat shot from under a throw pillow I lifted, I hit a high note that'd make any opera singer proud.

Millie leaned against the counter and hooted for all of five seconds before a second rodent sprang from the cabinet, launched itself across the countertop, onto the floor, and out the trailer door. But for that five-second interval, we would've been a duet.

"Let's get out of here," Millie pleaded. "I didn't sign up for hazardous duty."

"No argument here," I responded. "It'll take braver folks than us to tackle this job."

Once we were outside, we peeled off our gloves, tossed them into an overrunning open trash can, and headed back to the car. As she opened her door, Millie stopped.

"Ewwww!" she squawked. "There's a sheet of paper stuck to the bottom of my sneaker." With one hand on the door, she stuck her foot up and yelped, "Get it off!"

"Oh, my goodness," I sniped, walking around the car and bending down. "Why do I have to be the one to touch it? It's just paper and maybe a little chewing gum or..." I chose not to speculate any further.

"I don't want to think about it," Millie whined. "It's probably rat poop. Or worse."

"Hold still," I instructed as I slipped a fresh latex glove from my pocket. I gripped the edge of the paper and the whole nasty blob came loose.

"There," I sighed. "You're saved."

"It's a piece of a coloring book page," Millie noted. "But what's this?" she asked, pointing to a crayon scrawl at the bottom.

"Looks like a phone number," I said, beginning to get a bit excited. "Maybe this is the clue we've been looking for!"

"Call it," Millie insisted. "See who answers."

"No way," I told her. "If this number is connected with Ray

John's death and maybe even Jewel's disappearance, I don't want whoever's on the other end seeing my cell phone number on his caller I.D."

"Good point," Millie agreed. "Is there still a pay phone around anywhere?"

"Not that I can think of. But we could always borrow a business phone somewhere."

"Like at Bill's office?" Millie suggested.

"Or at Whiter Than Snow," I said. "It's a lot closer."

We opted to leave my car at the church and go straight to the laundromat. We'd barely gone half the distance when my cell phone rang out "Sweet Home Alabama." This was my ringtone for all callers except those I'd assigned special ringtones. The screen identified the caller as "Carrie Parker."

"Hi, Carrie," I began, but was quickly interrupted.

"A deputy come by here and told me they found Jewel's truck. Somebody set fire to it and they was a body inside it," Carrie's voice was broken and barely above a whisper.

"Oh, Carrie, I'm so sorry," I told her, motioning for Millie to pull over. "I'm with Millie. Hold on one second while I put you on speaker. Have they told you it's Jewel?"

"Uh-uh," Carrie responded, still whispering. "I don't see no point in tellin' the young'uns until we know somethin' for certain."

"I think that's a wise idea," Millie said. "Carrie, where did they find the truck?"

"Up in Bankhead Forest," she answered. "Winston County side of Smith Lake. That's a good 70 miles from here. What would she'd a-been doin' up there?"

"I don't know, Carrie," I told her. "Do you need us to come over?"

"Naw, I'll be all right, I reckon. I just wanted y'all to know. Keep prayin'. And pray that body ain't my daughter."

"We will," Millie and I both responded.

"And if you think of anything else we can do, call back and we'll take care of it," I assured her.

As soon as Carrie hung up, I placed a call to Daddy and told him about Carrie's sad news and about what we had found at the trailer. "We're going to the laundromat and use that phone to call the number," I told him.

"No!" Daddy barked. "What you're going to do is take that piece of paper straight to Detective Metz. That's possible evidence and you could get yourself into a lot of hot water and danger if you withhold it."

"Okay, okay," I griped. "I should have known better than to tell you before we did it."

Detective Metz wasn't at the station when I phoned, but he'd apparently told the dispatcher to put me through to his cell phone if I called – thank goodness for Daddy's cop connection. As soon as I told him about our find, he said to meet him at Milo's Hamburgers where he could grab lunch as we talked. Nobody had to ask me twice to get me to Milo's.

"It'll be an hour or so," I told him. "I'm on TV shortly, so I'll have to run do my segment first. Will one o'clock be okay?"

Metz grunted a "Yeah" and hung up.

We sped to the church and Millie slid to a halt beside my car. I jumped out, grabbed my clothes and makeup bag, and threw them into her back seat. We were at the station in record time. I made fast work of changing and repairing my makeup and then I was on the set, off the set, and back out the door. We made the parking lot of Milo's at 12:59. Metz was parked and waiting.

Milo Carlton opened his first hamburger joint in 1946 on the north side of Birmingham. Patrons couldn't get enough of his special sauce, and today there are more than a dozen locations scattered around Alabama. I ordered my usual cheeseburger with grilled onions, a side of fries, and sweet tea – another thing for which Milo's has become famous. Shop talk would have to wait until we'd finished.

As Metz crumpled his wrapper and pushed his tray aside, he did exactly what I'd expected: launched into a stern lecture about the risk Millie and I had taken, being in Jewel and Ray John's trailer. "What would you have done if that white Hyundai had shown up?" he questioned.

"Locked the door and called you," Millie responded.

"Uh, the door lock's broken," I reminder her.

"Well, we'd have stacked up furniture and barricaded the door and …"

Metz interrupted, holding up a hand for her to stop. "I don't know why I'm wasting my breath. You two are as mule-headed as Woody, and that mule-headedness cleared a lot of cases while he was on the job. Just be careful, ok? That's all I'm asking."

"Oh, we will," Millie promised. "Why, after Clarice told Judy she'd seen …"

I kicked her leg beneath the table and Millie let out a small yelp and stopped midsentence. But not soon enough.

"Seen what?" Metz asked, leaning across the table and giving us both a threatening look. "And who's this Clarice?"

"Oh, uh," I stammered, "Clarice is my neighbor. Really nice lady. Great cook."

"I don't sidetrack, Bates," Metz warned me. "What did this

Clarice see and when and where?"

I resigned myself to a full confession. "It was sometime Wednesday," I admitted. "She said she saw a small white car riding up and down our street. But that doesn't mean it was the same one," I added.

"Yeah, and Florida doesn't have any beaches," Metz grunted. "I don't suppose you've mentioned this to Woody, either, have you?"

I was beginning to get a bit defensive at this point. "Well, no, I didn't, Detective Metz. After all, why would I want to burden my elderly father with something that may or may not be worth worrying about?"

At that, Metz fairly snorted. "Yeah, right. Elderly." He started wagging a meaty finger under my nose. "Your daddy has invaluable years of experience. He can smell clues. And I know for a fact that he'll read you the riot act when he finds out you're withholding information. Trust me on this. I know. If you want him on this case, then tell him everything. Otherwise, you should never have dragged him into this mess in the first place."

"And," he added, "since I happen to be the person in charge of this investigation, it would be smart not to keep anything from me, either."

My red face let him know I'd gotten the message. And Millie at least had the decency to look a bit sheepish.

"I'll tell him," I promised. "And I'll let you know anything of importance that I find out or that happens."

"That's more like it," Metz nodded. "Now that we have all that out of the way, let's take a look at this phone number."

I slid the Ziploc bag across the table and Metz picked it up. "Hmmm," he muttered, "I don't recognize this area code. Let's go to my car and check this out."

I'd seen a couple of people doing the whisper and stare thing that often happens when they recognize me from my TV spot. Now one man was at Milo's front window gesticulating wildly for a lady, presumably his wife, to join him and see the action. Metz opened the back door of his unmarked police car and waited for me and Millie to get in.

Why can't they make unmarked cars look less conspicuous? I mean, between the plain exterior and a dashboard that looks like it came off the starship *Enterprise*, it's not exactly hard to spot one. And now every person in Milo's seemed to know that's what Millie and I were sitting in.

Metz pecked around on his onboard computer as Millie and I craned our necks to see the readout. "Puerto Rico," he said. "This is a Puerto Rico area code."

He punched a few more keys and mumbled as he scanned the screen. "Burner phone. Figures. But two can play that game," he added, giving us a wink and opening the glove compartment.

"Completely untraceable," he explained, holding up a cell phone.

❖

On the other side of the city, Jimmy Sarnecki sat on a stool in the diner ogling the cute little waitress – Emily, according to her name tag – who'd brought his order. He'd tried to start up a conversation, but she'd made some lame excuse about having other customers. She had to get off work sometime. And then he'd be waiting.

His phone rang. Correction. His other phone rang. The one The Collector had told him to get rid of after he'd taken care of that saucy little Fitzhugh chick. *Too bad she'd checked out before I got the information out of her,* he reflected. That hadn't made his boss too happy.

But like blowing money on a rental car, Jimmy had considered tossing a perfectly good phone a waste of good money. After all, it was next to impossible to trace that kind of burner phone, and he always liked to have a backup. Especially a free one.

The color drained from Jimmy's face as he sprang from his stool and ran for the doorway. What if The Collector was checking to see if he'd tossed the phone? Jimmy studied the number, but didn't recognize it. He swallowed hard, then answered.

You big dummy, thought Metz. Why hadn't he come up with a plan before calling the number? When he heard a quiet "Yeah?" on the other end of the phone, Metz started his ad lib, punching the speaker button and motioning for me and Millie to stay quiet.

"Who is this?" Metz said, intentionally sounding as gruff as possible.

"Who wants to know?" the weasly voice snapped back at him.

"Hey, man, be nice, ok?" Metz told him. "I believe I have something you want and we might can work a deal if you don't make me hang up this phone."

Seconds ticked by before the Weasel, as Metz had begun thinking of him, spoke again. "Whatcha got? And why do you think I'd be interested?"

"Let's say it's something Jewel Fitzhugh was nice enough to show me," Metz replied coolly. He could hear the intake of breath and knew he'd hooked him.

"Where you callin' from?" the Weasel asked him.

Metz prayed his bluff would work. "Why, I'm right here where you are, buddy. In good ol' Birmingham, Alabama."

Did this guy really know where he was? Nah, Jimmy thought. He was only guessing. Still, Jimmy could hardly believe his luck. He'd gone against The Man's orders twice now and instead of landing himself in hot water, he'd found a way to get his hands on that megabuck baseball card. Surely his boss would have to show him some greenback respect when he completed this deal singlehandedly.

"OK," Jimmy responded as he made his way across the parking lot. "I'm listening."

"Myself, I don't know much about baseball," Metz said in a friendly tone, "but I do know something's gotta be worth some serious coin for somebody to be willing to waste a couple of people over it."

Jimmy felt his face burning with rage. "You're behind the count already, man," Jimmy hissed through clinched teeth. "And one more ain't gonna be no problem."

"You threatening me, mister?" Metz continued as if that kind of talk didn't faze him.

"No threat," Jimmy assured him. "A promise. Unless you hand over the merchandise."

"Well, now, you've done gone and made me angry," the man said, his voice taking on just a hint of menace. "And that, my new source of income, is really gonna cost you."

Cool down, cool down, Jimmy warned himself. "What kind of coin are we talking?" Jimmy asked him.

"Oh, I'd say fifty G's oughta cover it," came the answer.

"Fifty G's!" Jimmy choked. He used an entire string of his favorite expletives as his closer.

"Temper, temper, my newfound friend," the voice warned him. "One more of those dirty little words and the price'll go up. Steeply."

"Ok, ok." *Don't get greedy,* Jimmy admonished himself. The offer was half what that Fitzhugh guy had been asking. The boss would have to be impressed when he completed this deal. And if he took this guy out in the process, so what? There might just be a

144

bonus for tying up another loose end.

"You meet me tonight," Metz continued, "under the viaduct…"

Jimmy interrupted. "No way, man. I tell you where and when. And I see the card before you see the coin. Got it?"

There was a pause and then the man responded: "You drive a hard bargain, but you've got yourself a deal. Now tell me how we can do business."

The old mill had served him well on several occasions, so Jimmy would use it as their meeting place. He started to name the location, then thought better of it. "You just be sittin' on ready," Jimmy told him. "I'll let you know where to go and when to be there."

Jimmy hit the "end call" symbol and grinned. He wasn't nearly as stupid as his mom had always said he was. This time, he had the upper hand and he'd use it to make his bones with The Collector and add a nice chunk to his retirement fund in the process. He strolled back into the diner and polished off his now cold meal with gusto. He peeled off a fifty and pressed it into Emily's hands.

"I had big plans for you tonight, sweetheart," he told her, leaning in and causing her to take a step backward. "But it looks like that'll have to wait 'til another time. I got business tonight, baby. But I'll be seeing you."

He sauntered out the door, smiling happily as he remembered the frightened look on Emily's teenage face.

Millie and I were still holding our corporate breath when the call ended. With a mumbled, "Hang on," Metz pecked around on his onboard computer before turning to us with a smug smile of satisfaction. "Got him," he said. Pointing to a pulsing dot on a grid on his computer screen, he explained, "That call pinged off this tower. If you ladies will kindly exit my ride, I've got a criminal to catch."

"Why can't we go with you?" I wheedled. "You're going to have to check that whole area, and you don't know who you're looking for or exactly where he was. Three pairs of legs can cover a lot more territory."

Metz sighed, started the engine, and threw the car in reverse. "True," he said. "And that guy's bound to be long gone by now, so it should be safe for you two to do a little asking around. Somebody may have noticed something."

Fifteen minutes later, we were standing in the parking lot of a rather seedy-looking strip mall. The shops bore the signage that defined most declining areas: a liquor store, a pawn shop, and a payday loan business. Along with these were a nail salon and a hair stylist, plus three eateries: Joanie's Diner, Happy Dragon Chinese, and Dave's Dogs.

"We were having lunch, and I'm betting the Weasel was, too," Metz said. "We'll each take a restaurant. Ask if any man got a call about 20 minutes ago."

"Probably only every other guy in all three restaurants," Millie said. "We've got to have more than that to go on."

Metz pulled at his bottom lip for a couple of seconds, then snapped his fingers. "He went outside. When the Weasel answered the phone, I could hear restaurant noises – you know what I mean."

"That's right," I interrupted. "I remember hearing a car door slam. He went out to the parking lot."

"You got it," Metz agreed. "Now, Millie, take Joanie's. Bates, check out Happy Dragon. I'll go to Dave's. If you find out anything – and I do mean anything – call my cell and I'll be right there."

Within five minutes, I'd attempted conversation with every employee in sight at Happy Dragon. Few spoke much English. All were eager to get away from me and back to their customers. Strike One.

At Dave's Dogs, Metz fared no better, although when he flashed his badge, an entire table of rough-looking teens slid out of their booth and bolted out the door. Strike Two.

Now it was all up to Millie. Bright pink "Joanie's" logo tees and khaki shorts must have been the uniform of the day because Millie saw four of these outfits bustling around the little diner. One, she noticed, seemed to be barking the most orders, so she pegged this leather-skinned blond as the manager or owner.

"Joanie?" Millie asked, approaching the woman as she was refilling an iced tea dispenser.

"Yeah, that's me," the lady answered. "Hang on one sec and I'll be right with you." In less than a minute, order pad in hand, she was standing in front of Millie.

"I'm assisting in a police investigation," Millie told her and saw Joanie's big blue eyes widen in response. "A man somewhere in this area received a phone call about twenty minutes ago, and I'm hoping you might remember somebody's phone ringing."

At that, Joanie fairly snorted. "Honey, I'm training a new cook, and we've been packed out. I wouldn't have noticed if every phone in here had been ringing. What's he look like?"

"Well, that's the problem," Millie told her. "We don't know. But you might have noticed his voice. It's grating. Whiny. I wish I had more I could tell you."

"And I wish I could help," Joanie answered. "Why's the police looking for him?"

"I can't tell you much," Millie lowered her voice, "but I can say that he's a very dangerous man."

"Is he some sort of pervert?" Joanie questioned.

"I don't really know anything about him," Millie answered,

148

"except that it's really important we find him."

"I've got a lot of ESPN," Joanie told her, watching the puzzled look on Millie's face. "It's a joke, hon. We had a customer come in here talking about having ESPN, and we thought he meant the TV channel, until he said he thought he was psychic."

"Anyway," Joanie continued, "I do depend on my gut a lot, and about the time you're talking about, one of my girls had a real slimeball for a customer. Her name's Emily. Park yourself on that end stool and I'll go get her."

Moments later, 17-year-old Emily Scarborough was seated beside Millie. Her dark brown hair draped down her back in a long single braid and her youthful face showed no signs of makeup, nor did it need it. She was a natural beauty displaying, at the moment, a very timid and nervous half-smile.

"Miss Joanie said you wanted to talk to me," Emily said softly.

"I do," Millie answered. "She said you had a creepy customer a little while ago. Do you mind telling me a little about him?"

As she spoke, Emily pulled a small cross necklace from inside her shirt and began to rub the cross between her fingers. "Sure," she responded. "He ordered the special – hamburger steak, mashed potatoes, and green beans – and sat right over there." She pointed to the stool at the opposite end of the counter, farthest from the entrance.

"Ok," Millie encouraged.

"He kept looking at me," Emily told her. "Watching me. Really creeped me out. And then when he got up to leave, he gave me this" – she pulled out the fifty and showed it to Millie – "and he got way too close to me and said, 'I had big plans for you tonight, sweetheart.' As soon as he left, I told Miss Joanie."

Millie tried to hide her disappointment. "Sounds like a weirdo for sure, Emily, but the guy I'm looking for received a phone call while he was here. I was hoping you might have been the one who waited on him."

Emily's eyes brightened. "Oh, but he did! I'm sorry. I didn't even think about that. Yes, his phone rang not long after I served him. He went out the door and was gone so long I was beginning to think that he'd left without paying. But next time I noticed, he was back on the stool finishing his lunch. After that is when he got in my face and said the scary stuff. And when he handed me that money," Emily shivered, "he petted my hand like we had something going." She shivered again. "I can't stand to think about it."

By now, Millie had punched in Metz's phone number and was counting the milliseconds until he answered. "Found him," Millie told him. "You and Judy come to Joanie's." Home run.

Millie slid her phone back into her pocket and hugged the startled young waitress. "You have no idea how important this is, Emily. A police officer will be coming through that door any second now, and he'll need to ask you some more questions. He looks big and tough, but between you and me, he's a teddy bear. And I'll be right here with you."

By the time Metz and I arrived, Millie and Emily had reseated themselves in the back corner booth, and Metz and I were able to slide in across from them. Emily was one smart young lady and her description of the Weasel was well detailed.

"I'd really like for you to come to the station and sit down with a sketch artist, Emily," Metz had told her, and she had readily agreed.

"When do you want me there?" Emily asked.

"Right now would be great," Metz told her. "The sooner we identify this guy, the sooner we catch him."

"Let me check with Joanie and see if I can leave before my shift ends," Emily responded.

A few minutes later, Emily returned to the booth with Joanie right alongside her. "I don't think you'll need Emily to I.D. this guy," Joanie told them. "I've got his sleazy little face on our security camera."

26

Metz used his phone to snap photos of Joanie's surveillance footage of the Weasel. Millie and I took the opportunity to take our own shots while we were at it. By the time we were headed back to Millie's car at Milo's, Officer Stanford had called with the news that the Weasel had been identified as one James Perry Sarnecki.

"And you'll never guess where his mama lives," Metz said, "so I hope you ladies won't mind a quick detour."

Not ten blocks from Joanie's, Metz pulled to the curb on a street of rundown rental properties. This neighborhood was known for drug deals, drive-by shootings, and all things illegal. As Metz let down his window and scanned the house numbers, Millie and I watched a scantily clad trio of women on the block ahead of us. One laughed raucously, waving a cigarette in the air and playfully pushing one of her companions. "Girl, please!" the woman cackled. "You crazy!"

Moments later, a silver Lexus pulled up beside the ladies and the threesome began vying for attention. The tallest one leaned into the car, then opened the door and climbed in. The other two clattered their six-inch heels over to a nearby bench to await their next opportunity.

Our gawking was interrupted by the sound of Metz's voice. "There it is," he said, pointing at a decrepit box-shaped bungalow several houses up and across from where we'd parked. An ancient coat of green paint had faded to a sickly gray-green and, like dead skin after a sunburn, the once-white trim remained only in patches.

"What now?" I whispered, as if Sarnecki or his mom might hear us.

"We'll take a leisurely lap around the block," Metz responded, "and see if we can see a white Hyundai parked anywhere around here." Turning around to stare at both of us, he added, "I believe you ladies might be familiar with that vehicle."

Lights and sirens wouldn't have made us any more conspicuous than Metz's unmarked car. By the time we'd rolled halfway up the block, the two working girls had waved away a potential customer and rushed into the burglar-barred mini-mart.

"I didn't see the Hyundai," Millie said after we'd covered the entire block and returned to our starting position.

"He's not home," Metz said, turning to face me and Millie, "so now might be a good time to have a chat with Mrs. Sarnecki. But on second thought," he said after a pause, "I better not spook him. We'll talk to her after we've got her boy in custody. And by 'we,' I don't mean you two. You ladies are going back to your car. I don't want you anywhere around here. Do you hear me?"

"Loud and clear, sir," I assured him. "The farther we are from this Sarnecki guy, the happier we'll be. Get us outta here."

Jimmy rattled around his basement apartment, antsy for darkness. He'd cleaned his Sig Sauer, his adrenaline pumping as he anticipated the night's adventure. After the phone call, he'd moved the Hyundai around to the back of the strip mall and walked home. Today was not the day for his mom to start yapping about needing her car back. Pretty soon she could have it and he'd be gone from this dump and riding in style. Once he got his hands on that baseball card.

Millie and I left Milo's and drove straight to the church so I could pick up my car. Metz had promised he'd let us know anything else he found out, but I figured I'd get better results and more details if I clued in my daddy.

"I'll be in the studio the rest of the afternoon," Millie called as I climbed into my Honda. "I want to know every detail the minute you find out anything new."

En route home, I called Daddy to fill him in on the latest. As usual, he was way ahead of me.

"Ray John's prints were all over the baseball card," Daddy added to the news I thought I was sharing.

"Do you think Sarnecki killed Ray John?" I responded.

"Not necessarily," Daddy cautioned, "but there's some connection between the card, Sarnecki, and Ray John."

"True," I said. "Now we have to hope and pray that Sarnecki calls Metz back and sets up a meet soon."

"Oh, he will," Daddy assured me. "Greed has a way of outweighing caution. He's gonna want to get his hands on that card as soon as possible."

Back at home, I took my laptop out onto the screened porch and starting working on my website. There were online deals to be posted, my daily Bible study, and a ton of Facebook messages and emails to answer. As I pounded the keyboard, my cell phone chirped, signaling a text message. Millie wanted to know if I'd heard from Metz.

"Not one word," I spoke into the phone. Watching my response appear on the phone, I groaned. Good ol' voice recognition. It'd typed "Not one wad." I corrected the sentence and hit the send arrow.

When I'd first starting using the voice software to let my phone type my messages, I'd assumed it would actually type what I was saying. Wrong. After I'd sent Gwen a message inviting her to ride to "Fart Payne" with me for a speaking engagement, I'd learned my lesson. The city was Fort Payne. Voice rec is still learning to translate my Southern accent.

Seconds after I turned back to my laptop, my phone chirped again. This time, it was Larry. "Hi, hon. How about I stop and pick us up some supper?" This was followed by a row of multi-colored hearts.

"How about I make chicken kabobs with rice and salad," I spoke into the phone. This time the voice rec got it right.

"Sounds perfect. Just like you," came Larry's response. Boy, he was hungry, slathering it on that thick.

"Aren't you the sweet one," I responded, adding an emoji of a kissing couple. I smiled and thought how true the old saying was about the key to a man's heart being through his stomach. At least, that was sure true in Larry's case.

"See you in about an hour," Larry answered.

I'd already loaded skewers with chicken, pineapple, onion, and bell pepper and had sealed them in gallon Ziploc bags to marinate in a blend of zesty Italian dressing, Worcestershire sauce, and a touch of garlic powder. I'd add some fresh ground black pepper once I got them on the grill. As I settled my tray of goodies onto the grill's sideboard, I felt a vibration in my hip pocket, followed by very faint notes of "My Dad."

Snatching out my phone, I said, "You really are a detective. You knew I was putting food on the grill before I even got started."

"Very funny," Daddy retorted. "I happen to be having supper with one of the lovely ladies of Last Gasp."

"Do tell," I teased. "And who is the lucky recipient of your charms this evening?" Truth be told, I was both pleased and surprised. Mother was in heaven, and who was I to resent Daddy enjoying a little female companionship?

"Helen Brooks," Daddy answered. "She's the only female in the whole complex who hasn't been plying me with food and coming up with lame excuses for me to come into her apartment."

It was at this point that I let out a very unladylike snort. "She hasn't invited you in to see her etchings?" By now, I was outright cackling.

"No, she has not," Daddy said, forcing himself not to laugh. "Ever since I moved in here, the maintenance men have apparently started slacking off because I'm constantly asked to change light bulbs, unclog sinks, and you'd be amazed how many times I've been asked to check under a bed for everything from spiders to dang near boa constrictors."

"And not a one of them has managed to get their hooks in you?" I asked.

"No way," Daddy said. "I'm an old man with old-fashioned ideas. I want to do the pursuing. That's what attracted me to Helen."

"What? The fact that she ignored you?" I snickered.

"The fact that she behaved like a lady," came his rejoinder.

"You mean she didn't sit across the dining room batting her

157

eyelashes and giving you those 'come hither' looks?" I asked him.

"You can be a real pain sometimes, dear daughter," Daddy said.

"OK, I won't say another word," I promised.

"Then I'll get to the business at hand," Daddy said. "Sarnecki called Metz. The meet's going down at midnight."

"What is it with criminals and midnight?" I asked Larry as we enjoyed our supper on the screened porch.

"Got me," he answered. "I like to get in the bed at a decent hour. Me, I'd want my clandestine rendezvous around 9:00 or 9:30. That way, if I hurried, I'd be home for the ten o'clock news."

"You'd be a very good criminal, I'm sure," I assured him, leaning over and kissing his cheek. "If you put your mind to it."

"Thank you, sweetie," he responded. "I'd give it my best."

"I'm a bit disappointed with Daddy, though," I said.

"Why?" Larry asked, his eyebrows raising in surprise. "Surely you're not upset about him dating."

"No! Not at all," I promised. "But he absolutely refused to tell me where Metz said he was meeting Sarnecki."

"That's because he knew he couldn't trust you to stay out of it," Larry answered.

"Like I'd be crazy enough to stick my nose into a police operation," I said, trying my best to appear insulted.

"Your dad knows you as well as I do," Larry said. "That information would be far too tempting if you had it."

"And thank you for your support!" I huffed.

Larry shrugged and chucked me lightly on the shoulder with his fist. "We just know you. That's all I'm saying."

We'd gone to bed around 10:30, and I was still wide awake as Larry lay beside me sawing logs. No, make that giant sequoia trees. I was going to need my earplugs and sound machine tonight.

A much softer rumbling sound turned my attention to the nightstand where my phone was doing a silent jitterbug across the surface. I snatched it up, threw back the covers, and padded through the bathroom into our walk-in closet.

Before I could get "hello" out of my mouth, Millie whispered excitedly into the phone, "I've got the info!"

"What info?" I whispered back, wondering why on earth I was whispering when a tornado siren would be impossible to hear above all the racket going on in the bedroom.

"The meeting place. Midnight at Cheney's Mill in Brookside."

"Cheney's Mill?" I queried.

"Yeah, you know, the one before you get to the closed-off road that used to go up to Coalburg Mines. On Five-Mile Creek."

"How'd you …" I began, but Millie interrupted.

"Kiki."

"But how'd Kiki …" Interrupted again.

"Remember, her cousin Walter works with Metz," Millie explained. "She said it was going to cost me a family portrait in oil. But it was worth it."

"But Coalburg's outside Metz's jurisdiction, isn't it?" I questioned.

"So's Carrie's house. And the trailer park. This thing has crossed so many jurisdictional lines that Metz has gotten the okay to follow it wherever it leads. In exchange, he's supposedly keeping all the other jurisdictions in the loop."

"But knowing him, he won't report to them until after all the dust settles," I said. "Methinks Detective Metz could use some backup."

Thirty minutes later, I'd picked up Millie by her mailbox and we were headed toward Cheney's Mill. I glanced over at her and immediately started snickering.

"Oh, like you look any better," Millie snapped. Her silver locks were stuffed beneath a black knit cap, and her face was smeared with shoe polish or possibly soot. Her top and pants were black, as well as her sneakers.

"I'm not the one with my face smeared with goop," I told her. "I may be dressed like you, but I brought a full-face ski cap. Nothing but my eyes will be showing. No need for the facial gunk." I looked over again and laughed even harder.

"So what's the plan?" she asked, ignoring my commentary.

"I don't know," I told her. "We'll figure it out when we get there."

After turning off onto the dirt road, I switched off the headlights and used only the parking lights and moonlight to navigate. "It's a quarter 'til midnight. We're just in time," I whispered. "There's Metz's car up ahead. We'd better park back here and walk the rest of the way."

Spotting a fairly safe-looking spot a few feet ahead, I eased my trusty Fit into the knee-high weeds, cut the engine, and reached to shut off the interior light. "OK," I said, handing Millie my bug repellent, "drown yourself in this, get your flashlight, and let's get going. I brought us a couple of weapons, too," I added, patting a black bag I'd pulled from the back floorboard.

"I don't know how to use a gun," Millie hissed.

"Don't worry," I whispered back. "You'll know how to use this, I promise."

As we crept along the edge of the road, clouds scudded across the sky, and an occasional flash of heat lightning zigzagged in the distance. Somewhere in the woods to our right, an owl hooted.

Myriads of insects buzzed and hummed all around us as lightning bugs winked their lights off and on like neon signs on the fritz. From a hundred or so feet to our left came the babbling of Five-Mile Creek, accompanied by a chorus of bullfrogs. Anyone who thinks the woods are quiet has never been in them at night.

"Does Bill know where you are?" I whispered.

"Are you kidding?" Millie answered. "He's out like a light."

"So's Larry," I said. "I did leave a note, just in case we get into any trouble."

"Like he's going to wake up and find it?"

"I put it where I know he will. I taped it to the toilet lid."

"Smart," Millie said. "I should've thought of that."

"Shhh," I warned. "Switch your light off and listen."

The bullfrogs had quieted as a soft thud, followed by a groan, came from the direction of the creek bank. Silently pointing toward the noise, I darted across the road and into the waist-high weeds. Millie followed behind me.

About halfway to the creek bank, I signaled a stop and we froze in place, listening again. Nothing. It was like the whole woods had suddenly gone silent. Another minute of crouched-over walking and we could make out a human-shaped lump on the ground in the clearing ahead of us.

Millie stifled a scream. I whirled and gave her my best glare – for all the good it did in the darkness.

Signaling her to stay put, I got down on all fours and crawled toward the body. Warm ooze coated the man's neck as I felt for a pulse in his carotid artery. It was there. Thready, but he had a heartbeat. I sat up and flipped on my flashlight, shielding it with my blood-smeared hand.

Millie crept up beside me. "It's Walter," she mouthed. "Kiki's cousin. He must have come with Metz as backup."

163

A few more seconds of examination and we found the source of the blood and the thud: a huge tree limb lay beside Walter's body. His attacker had used it to render him unconscious.

Whipping out my phone, I scrolled to Art's number and texted "Send EMTs to cheneys mill brookside." As an afterthought, I added, "and police. lots of them." Now that Art was on the mend from his own head injury, I knew he'd be back to his usual night owl routine and would see the message as soon as I sent it.

Leaning into Millie's ear, I whispered, "You stay with Walter. I'm going on ahead."

Her hand squeezed my arm like a vise grip as she hissed back, "Are you insane? I'm not staying here by myself."

"OK," I answered, jerking my arm free and wincing at the pain. "All heck is going to break loose when the cavalry arrives anyway. We'll show them where to find Walter then. Come on."

We belly-crawled out to the edge of the weeds before rising to half-crouches and moving forward. Using only the moonlight and occasional lightning flash to see, we worked our way toward the ruins of Cheney's Mill.

In the late 1880s, the Cheney family had been one of the few non-Slovaks to come to the area that was eventually incorporated into the town of Brookside along Five-Mile Creek. Eastern Europeans, mainly Slovaks, flocked in to work the coal mines, while Hiram Cheney saw an opportunity to make money using the free energy of Five-Mile Creek to power his grist mill. Cotton may have been king, but corn was a, literally, growing commodity, and Cheney's decision was a wise one.

Tonight, the outline of the decrepit mill loomed ahead of us like Frankenstein's castle. At the nearest standing wall, I motioned for Millie to go left while I went right. All I got for my effort was a fierce shake of her head and her hand shooting out to once again vise-grip my arm.

After wrenching my arm from the claws of Mrs. Chicken, we began a slow circuit around the building. Turning the corner to the back side, we could see what was left of the giant waterwheel that had once turned the grinding stones. That was when we heard the voice of the Weasel.

"Ain't nobody gonna rip off ol' Jimmy," he was saying. "Not and get away with it."

"Now hold on," a second person said. Metz. He was doing his best to sound calm, but there was definitely an edge to his voice.

"Now what?" Millie mouthed into my ear.

"Stay here. I'm going in a little closer," I answered. "And hang onto this," I added, handing her one of my secret weapons.

For once, she didn't argue. The creek bank had eroded over the years, and what had once been a five- or six-foot wide strip of land between the back wall of the mill and the water was now a narrow ledge with some spots washed out all the way up to the wall itself.

I prayed not to plunge off into the river as I negotiated the washouts, stretching my short legs as far as they could go to reach across some of the chasms. Beside me, the once gentle slosh of Five-Mile Creek now sounded like the sucking mouth of the sea monster Charybdis preparing a whirlpool to pull me in and devour me.

As I neared the waterwheel, I could see a glimmer of light through a gaping hole where the waterwheel's drive shaft disappeared into the building. With my left shoulder firmly pressed against the wall, I eased forward, mindful of debris and loose stones that could send me plummeting down the riverbank.

166

"Hey, I'm not greedy," Metz was saying. "Let's make it twenty-five G's and call it a night."

Sarnecki snorted. "You really think you're walking away from here with anything? You really think you're walking away from here at all? No, man, I got other plans for you."

"I don't suppose it would help to tell you I'm a cop," Metz began. "I'm just going to ease my hand into my pocket and show you my shield."

"And I'm just gonna put a hole in you if you move," Sarnecki responded.

"Look, buddy," Metz tried again. "My partner has you covered. You'll make this a lot easier on yourself if you put that gun down right now."

"Your partner," Sarnecki informed Metz, "is taking a little nap. Maybe even a permanent one."

"Why, you …" Metz must have moved. A shot rang out, followed by a loud scream. Was it me? I was so terrified I wasn't certain.

Feet pounded across the floorboards and Sarnecki was suddenly outside the building and less than twenty feet from where I was standing. "Who's out there?" Sarnecki bellowed.

His head swiveled left and, in that split second, I dropped onto my belly and put my face to the ground, shaking uncontrollably. I raised my head just enough to see him turn my way. That's when the second shot exploded.

The next thing I remember was sliding into the water. Was I

dead? Was I drowning? I was so scared, I wasn't sure. That was
when it occurred to me that I couldn't be dead and scared at the
same time. At least, I don't think I could. Treading water and
trying not to panic, I started feeling around my body for holes or
blood or any other signs of injury.

That was when the third shot hit the water right beside me. No,
I was definitely alive and had plans to stay that way. I ducked
under, tore off my ski mask, and starting swimming for all I was
worth, frantically praying I was headed downstream away from
Sarnecki.

My lungs bursting, I swam until I had no choice but to surface
for air. When I did, the first sound I heard was Sarnecki.

The beam of a powerful flashlight blinded me and I heard the
Weasel say, "Sayonara, whoever you are."

I wanted to duck back underwater, but I was frozen in terror.
I thought of Larry snoozing away at home. I thought of my dad. I
thought of my son and his family far away on the mission fields of
Uganda. And it was then that inexplicable peace flooded over me.
I knew, whether he killed me or not, I was going to be all right.

The words of 2 Timothy 1:12 came to me as sharply and
clearly as if I were reading them from my Bible: "I know whom I
have believed, and am persuaded that he is able to keep that which
I have committed unto him against that day."

Maybe this was "that day." If it was, I was ready. I treaded
water and waited.

But instead of another gunshot, I heard a howl of pain. The

blinding beam cut a swath across the sky and splashed into the water. I watched the glow sink quickly, then disappear.

I recognized the sufferer as Sarnecki – I could tell by the number of swear words he managed to get out between cries of pain. What on earth had happened?

A bigger splash was followed by Millie's calling to me as she swam toward me. "Are you hit? Judy! Judy! Speak to me!"

"I'm fine!" I called back. "What happened to Sarnecki?" By now, his cries were absolutely unearthly.

"I used your secret weapon," Millie sputtered as she finally reached me.

"You go, girl," I said before grabbing her in a hug that took us both underwater.

We surfaced to a cacophony of sirens, punctuated by shrieks and cursing from the agonizing Sarnecki. Millie made it up the bank ahead of me and extended a hand to haul me out.

"Metz!" we both yelped at the same time.

We scrambled back up the creek bank, jumping over the washouts and rushing into the mill. Metz lay on the floor, blood pooling beside him.

"Metz!" I called, dropping to my knees.

Millie knelt beside me. "Talk to me, Metz!" she pleaded.

His lips parted and his eyes opened for the briefest moment. "I told you two to steer clear of all this," he said, a goofy grin curling his lips before he winced in pain.

"Where'd he hit you?" I asked, looking him over for the source

169

of the blood.

"My shoulder," he wheezed. "Hurts like, uh, heck, but I'll be okay."

"Paramedics are here," Millie told him. "I'll go show them where the patients are."

At this, Metz began struggling to sit up. "Walter," he said. "What about Walter?"

"Sarnecki gave him a hard wallop with a tree limb, but he was still breathing when we left him," I assured Metz. "Lie still while I get you some help."

Making my way through the building and out the front, I stepped into utter pandemonium. Squad cars were everywhere. A half dozen ambulances were lined up, and maneuvering their way in between all that were the running figures of Larry and Bill.

"Honey, are you all right?" Larry grabbed me, his voice shaking with emotion.

"I'm fine, really," I promised. "Just a little wet."

"Where's Millie?" Bill demanded, equally upset.

"I'm right here, Bill," she called, jogging from upstream where she'd been directing EMTs to Walter.

At some point during our happy reunion, a couple of paramedics were kind enough to drape me and Millie with blankets. I hadn't even realized how hard I'd been shivering. How much was chill and how much was shock and exhaustion, I didn't know.

"So," I said, smiling up into Larry's big brown eyes, "Did you find my note or did Art call you?"

"I found the note," Larry answered, grinning in spite of his concern. "That was pretty slick thinking to put it there."

"I thought so," I mumbled, snuggling into his nice warm chest.

29

Excitement always makes me hungry, so I convinced Larry to make a stop at Waffle House. Bill and Millie agreed to join us. "After all," I pointed out, "it's practically breakfast time."

"Okay," Larry said, "but if any of your fans see you, they're going to be shocked."

"And who's going to be out at this hour?" I challenged. "We'll probably be the only customers in the building."

Wrong. Waffle House was packed, and as my shoes made squishing noises across the floor, two tables full of ladies started to wave and call out, "Bargainomics Lady! Hey! What happened to you?" Larry was right, as usual.

The rest of our group took a seat, and I told Larry to order me my fave: a plate of hash browns scattered, smothered, covered, chunked, topped, and diced. Translated, that's hash browns with onions, cheese, ham, chili, and diced tomatoes. I made my way over to the ladies.

They appeared to run the gamut from early twenties to senior citizens. "What are y'all doing out at this hour of the night?" I asked. "Or should I say morning?"

"We're the Thursday Night Rollers," a fortyish brunette spoke up. "We bowl in the midnight league at Valley Lanes. Better question, though," she said, eyeing me from top to bottom, "is what in the world have you been doing?"

"Ladies, it's a long story, and I imagine you'll see it all on the news the next day or two. Meanwhile, I'm gonna have to leave you in suspense." Eight disappointed faces stared back at me.

"But tell you what," I added. "You show me the kindness of not taking any photos with those cell phones," I said, nodding toward electronic gadgets scattered all over their tables, "and I'll send every one of you a copy of my new book for free. Deal?"

"Deal!" they chorused. And the brunette whipped out a pen and began writing down all their names and addresses on a napkin.

I had to have taken a shower before falling into bed, but the next thing I recall was waking up with a more-than-mild urge to tinkle. I reached across the bed and felt nothing but empty pillow where Larry's head had lain. Good heavens! Looking at the clock, I could see why he was up and also why I needed a bathroom so badly. It was almost noon!

I stopped short of the toilet as I saw the note in big red letters taped to the upraised lid. "I'm liking your message board," it read. "I'm out in the garage." He'd added a heart to the end of his message.

When I walked onto the screened porch, Daddy greeted me from the driveway using his very sweetest bellow. "If you think you're too old for me to tan your hide, you've got another think coming! Larry told me everything that happened, and you better not ever pull a stunt like that again."

"Ah, c'mon," I cajoled, seating myself on the porch swing and patting the empty spot beside me. "I'm fine. Everybody's fine. And, best of all, we even got the bad guy."

Daddy harrumphed a couple of times, but he finally came in and sat down. "You took a big risk, young lady," he said, pointing a finger within an inch of my nose.

"I'm just tickled to hear somebody call me 'young lady'," I teased, putting an arm around his shoulder. "What do I have to do to hear it again?"

"You better not even think about it," Daddy answered.

"Wouldn't dare," I promised, my fingers firmly crossed on both hands.

"If you two have settled your differences," Larry spoke through the screen, "I'm about to throw some steaks on the grill. Any volunteers to bake us some potatoes and throw together a salad?"

Both our hands went up, and Daddy and I hugged and declared a truce before scurrying off to the kitchen. I buttered a few slices of barbecue bread and Daddy took them out to Larry, who added garlic powder before placing them on the grill. A few minutes later, the three of us were seated around the porch table, chowing down on the best steaks in the universe. Larry is a true artist when it comes to steak-grilling.

Later that afternoon, Millie and Bill rolled up in the driveway. Daddy had gone to the hospital to visit Metz and Walter, and Larry and I were sitting on the swing absorbed in a crossword puzzle. After the lunch we'd had – not to mention the late night/early morning breakfast – we'd agreed we'd had more than enough food for one day.

However, our neighbor Clarice had brought over one of her mouthwatering sugarless peanut butter pies, so we decided to eat a slice of that and call it supper. I'd phoned and invited Millie and Bill to join us.

Sitting around the table scraping the last of the crumbs from our dishes, Larry announced, "Bill and I both need to hear the whole story again from the top. You two were exhausted when we talked at Waffle House, and I'll bet you left out a lot of the details. Now let's hear it. And leave no stone unturned."

So Millie and I took turns narrating the entire night's events, starting with Millie's phone call and going all the way through to when Larry, Bill, and the cavalry arrived.

"But one thing you still haven't explained," Bill said, looking at Millie. "You've repeatedly said, 'I took him out,' and you've both talked about Judy's secret weapon, but neither of you have told us what it was."

Millie and I looked at each other and grinned. "Remember when Daddy did that stint with the bomb squad..." I started.

"Whoa!" Larry said. "Don't tell me you used some kind of explosive?"

At this, Millie and I collapsed in a fit of laughter. "No, I'm just messin' with you, sweetie," I assured him.

"Hornet spray," Millie blurted. "I used hornet spray."

"You're kidding me!" Bill said, looking at his wife in amazement.

"Nope. That stuff'll shoot about twenty feet, so while the Weasel – that's Sarnecki – was focused on shooting Judy, I snuck up and shot him. Right in the eyeballs."

"You've never heard such a caterwauling in all your life!" I added.

"It must have been something," Larry said. "We only heard the tail-end as they were loading him onto the stretcher, but he sounded like he was in some kind of mortal pain, for sure."

"I gotta say, though," he continued, reaching over and squeezing my hand. "That was some pretty sharp thinking. I just don't want you two to get in the habit of pulling crazy stunts like that, you hear me?"

"Oh, we hear you," I said, nudging Millie's foot under the table. "Don't we, cuz?"

"We do," Millie promised.

My phone chirped, and I picked it up and checked the message. It was Daddy.

"Daddy says Sarnecki isn't talking," I told everyone after I'd read the text. "And Metz is griping at everybody that walks into the room, which means he's doing great. Docs will probably let him go home tomorrow."

"With a gunshot wound?" Bill questioned.

"It was a through-and-through," I explained. "It didn't do any serious damage. He'll just be really sore for a while."

"And on desk duty and miserable," Larry added.

"But what about Walter?" Millie asked.

"Daddy said he's been released. Miraculously, there was no concussion. They only kept him overnight for observation. He has a few stitches and a headache, but that's about it. I'd say everybody was really lucky," I concluded.

"Luck has nothing to do with it," Larry said. "And you know that as well as I do."

"True. I misspoke," I admitted. "The Lord had His hand on both those guys."

"And you girls, too," Bill added, reaching for Millie's hand across the table.

"Amen," we all agreed in unison.

177

30

Saturday morning. Millie and I were on our way to Carrie's. Rosa had found volunteers to fill in for me and Millie at Whiter Than Snow on Friday, and today Carlos offered to personally keep an eye on Ray Ray, Sissy, and Nubbin while we took Carrie for a makeover.

"You ready to go?" I called through the screen door. I could see Carrie herding her grandkids before her across the kitchen floor.

"I'm as nervous as a long-tailed cat in a room full of rockers, but I'm kinda excited, too," Carrie admitted. "Let's get this show on the road!"

Less than an hour later, the three of us were walking into Bevill State Community College's School of Cosmetology. Normally, the Cosmetology Department was closed on Saturdays, but when Kiki told her instructor about Carrie, she'd offered to help treat us to a private pampering session.

Carrie was seated in the chair of stylist-in-training Lisa Noles from our Bible study class at Whiter Than Snow. Thanks to Kiki's encouragement, she'd recently enrolled in the school and had just started classes.

"I really appreciate y'all trusting me with Miss Carrie," Lisa said. "She's gonna look like a movie star when we get done with her."

"Oh, Lordy," Carrie mumbled.

"Don't you worry one bit, honey," Lisa promised. "My instructor will be with me every step of the way. Let's get you into the shampoo chair for starters."

"Looks like you don't need us standing around in your way," I told Lisa. "So we'll treat ourselves to mani-pedis while we're waiting on Carrie." With that, Millie and I crossed the hall to where Kiki Roberts had just finished Rosa Moncada's pedicure.

"Looks like old home week around here," Millie teased as Rosa wiggled her newly painted toenails.

"It is!" Rosa responded, standing and hobbling barefoot with foam spacers between her toes, to give us each a hug. "Kiki is wonderful. She will make you feel like royalty."

"And I need one of you to get your royal fanny over into this chair," Kiki called, "and let's get this party started."

"I'm going to go supervise Lisa while you work on Judy," Millie announced.

"No, girl, that ain't happenin'," Kiki shook her head. "You let Lisa worry about Carrie. She knows what she's doing. You get yourself in the chair next to Judy, and Bree is gonna take care of you."

"Kiki, are you sure you should still be in class?" I asked. "I mean, you look like you could pop at any second."

"Believe me, being in class is a lot easier than chasing my two boys around. You take a seat and stop worryin' about me. I'm finer than frog hair," Kiki assured me.

So while Carrie's transformation was taking place across the hall, Millie and I were kicked back in comfy chairs and, just as Rosa had said, being treated like royalty. First, our feet were placed in jetted foot basins of warm water. After that, I can only assume Millie was getting the same treatment I was, because my eyes were closed and I was oblivious to anything else going on around me.

Kiki lifted one foot at a time from the water and gently toweled it dry. With her hands slathered in lotion, she began massaging my foot and lower leg. A huge smile must have appeared on my face because Kiki stopped massaging and said, "What you grinnin' about?"

I shook myself from my reverie and opened my eyes. "I was thinking about how Carrie is going to react to all this. She's never had anyone pamper her in any way."

"Well, that's about to change," Kiki responded, diving back into her work with both hands.

I thought of all the other areas of Carrie's life that were also changing.

I'd brought my favorite pale pink polish which Kiki examined and approved. After my toes were gleaming perfect, we moved over to her table for my manicure. More soaking, more massaging, and a heap of luxury later, and I was polished to perfection.

"Kiki, you are absolutely amazing!" I told her. "No salon could have done a better job." I reached across for a hug, but Kiki threw up a hand and quickly backed away.

"Don't you be touchin' me with those nails," she ordered. "They're supposed to be good and dry now, but let's not take any chances. Sit over there and behave yourself for a few more minutes."

"Yeah. What she said." Millie grinned and fluttered her crimson fingernails in my direction. "I'd say Bree did a fine job, too."

"She sure did," I agreed. And to back up our bragging, we both left sizable tips for our beautifiers.

As we headed back across the hall, Lisa appeared in the doorway. "Hang on a sec," she told us, holding up one finger and peering back behind her. "OK, I think we're ready."

"Wow!" Millie and I both blurted.

Gone was Carrie's long, slicked-back ponytail. Her hair now fell in a short swingy style that turned under just below the neckline and curved flatteringly toward her face. Her once lifeless brown hair now gleamed with streaks of soft, natural-looking

181

blond.

And her face! With her instructor's guidance and Carrie's permission, Lisa had applied a delicate layer of foundation, a neutral-toned eye shadow, and the very slightest amount of mascara. Carrie Parker was stunning.

"My hair feels good," Carrie said, shyly gazing at her reflection in the mirror.

"You look amazing," I told her. And I meant it. "As soon as you get your mani-pedi, me, you, Millie, and Rosa have got some shopping to do!"

We needed energy for what we were about to undertake next, so we decided to fortify ourselves with lunch at Dupree's, a treat that almost sent Carrie into orbit.

"Now what did you call what y'all ordered me?" Carrie asked after we were back in the car.

"Herb-encrusted halibut with wild rice pilaf," Millie told her.

"In other words, Carrie, fancy fish and rice," I said.

"It was fancy, all right," she agreed. "And real good, too."

"Millie and Judy were the first ones to introduce me to Dupree's," Rosa told Carrie. "Now Carlos and I try to have lunch there at least once a month."

"We'll have to do this again soon," Millie said. "Meanwhile, our first stop is Macy's."

"Mercy, y'all," Carrie protested. "I can't afford no Macy's clothes. I was thinking we'd be going to a thrift store or somethin'."

"Not this time, ma'am," I responded. "And besides, remember who you're shopping with. Macy's has a huge sale on right now. We're going to find you bargains galore!"

And that we did. Overwhelmed, Carrie finally parked herself on the bench in her dressing room and simply waited for the next batch of clothes to be lowered over the doorway. She'd put on an outfit, then open the door and let us inspect her before going back in to try on the next one.

"I can't believe I'm gettin' all these things for m'self," Carrie said as she did a slow turn in front of the full-length mirror. "I can't tell y'all how much I appreciate y'all helpin' me like this."

"We're glad to do it," Millie assured her. "And we need you to be one hundred percent honest about what you like and don't like. It doesn't matter how cute Judy or I think something is. We want you to pick out the things you really like. This is your money and your choices. We're only covering this shopping spree until the buyer of your baseball card comes through."

"My money," Carrie said, lowering her voice. "Ain't that somethin'? We got to get some things for the young'uns, too."

"That's another day's shopping," I told her. "Today, Mrs. Parker, is all about you." I punctuated my statement with a little bow and curtsy.

The next and final outfit Carrie tried on was white capris with a white camisole and a bright chiffon top splashed with pink, blue, green, yellow, and white. Millie ran over to the shoe department and came back with white patent sandals that looked as cute as a bug with Carrie's bright pink toenails. This time, when Carrie walked out of the dressing room, even our sales clerk Cassandra stopped to ooh and aah at our fashion plate.

"Leave it on," Rosa insisted. "We'll get Cassandra to ring it up and cut the tags off for us."

"No problem," Cassandra responded. "And I'll put your old clothes in a separate bag from your purchases."

"Probably ought to burn 'em," Carrie said. "Lands, I didn't realize how old fogey I looked until you girls got me all decked out from top to bottom. I'm liable to go home and dump out my whole closet!"

We all had a good laugh at that idea and then we gathered up Carrie's final selections and lugged them all to the register. With the coupon from my phone and the extra forty percent off on the clearance merchandise, we waltzed out of Macy's with more than five hundred dollars in outfits for just under a hundred dollars. That was impressive shopping, even for the Bargainomics Lady.

We dropped Carrie and Rosa at Rosa's house, where Carlos was playing a game of catch with Ray Ray while Sissy and Nubbin sat on the front stoop eating ice cream cones.

"Mercy," chuckled Carrie as she exited the car, "that ice cream looks to be meltin' 'bout twice as fast as those young'uns is eatin' it."

"Yes," said Rosa. "We'll get them cleaned up before we take you home."

"I don't have the words to tell you how much I appreciate everything y'all have done for me," Carrie said in a voice choked with emotion.

"We're happy to help," Millie and I assured her, and Rosa added a hug and a nod of agreement.

We waved to the kids, Carrie, and the Moncadas as Millie pulled away from the curb. "I don't know about you, cuz, but I've had enough togetherness and excitement to last me a while."

"I couldn't agree more," Millie replied. "I need some time in my studio and, hopefully, Bill and I can have this evening to ourselves and maybe do something mildly adventurous after church tomorrow."

"I think Larry and I will run up to the lake. Might even go up this evening and spend the night."

Larry appeared from the garage just as I closed the car door and waved goodbye to Millie.

"How about we ride up to the Old Cookstove for supper?" he suggested. The Cookstove was a Mennonite restaurant not too far from the lake and with the best and most home-cooked food choices of any place we'd ever eaten.

"And," he added, "I thought we could come back by the lake

and spend the night. It's only an hour's drive to church from there."

"You," I said, walking to him and wrapping my arms around his neck, "are a man after my own heart."

"And I thought I already had it," he responded.

"You do," I told him. And we stood on the driveway and kissed like crazy newlyweds.

31

Daddy and Helen were coming for Sunday lunch, so before Larry and I had left for the Cookstove, I had thrown a roast and veggies into the slow cooker and set it to cook on low overnight. I'd also transferred cornbread and cake layers from the freezer to the fridge so they'd be thawed by the time we got home from church. Then it'd only take a few minutes to warm the cornbread and ice the cake.

In the choir, Millie's eyes were fairly dancing as she leaned in and whispered, "I've got news, and you'll never guess what it is."

"You're pregnant," I dead-panned. "Congratulations."

"Very funny," she said, jabbing me with her elbow. "Bill has decided he's retiring! And guess what else?" She could hardly contain herself. "Oh, forget the guessing. Bill said we'd go to Norway with you and Larry. That is, if we're still invited."

"Are you kidding me!" I cheered. "Do you realize how many years we've been trying to get y'all to go with us? You're going to love it! I can't wait to tell Per and Iren. They're going to be so happy!"

Guys never seem to express enthusiasm like women, but for a guy, Larry was pretty pumped when I told him Bill had finally agreed to visit Norway. As I babbled on about all the places I wanted them to see and the things I wanted us to do, Larry went out on the porch to set the table.

Meanwhile, I opened a tub of frosting and slathered my now thawed cake layers. Wrapping the cornbread in a bread cloth, I popped it into the microwave in preparation for Daddy and Helen's arrival. Larry reappeared and got out the food processor to whip up some slaw. With a little prior planning, Sunday lunch was hardly any effort at all.

A few minutes later, everything was ready and waiting when Daddy's '56 came to halt on the driveway.

"They're here!" I called to Larry, leaning over the sink to peer out the kitchen window. "He's going around the car to open her door. Oh, my goodness! He's holding her hand."

"And thank you for the play-by-play," Larry said, shooing me away from the window. "You remind me of your mother when we were dating."

"Hey, at least I didn't go out to the car to meet them," I countered.

"I think your mom kept an egg timer handy," Larry declared. "If we weren't out of the car and in the house within three minutes, she was tapping on my window."

"Yep, and we still got to fog up that Fairlane's windows a time or two, didn't we?" I teased, swatting him playfully with a dish towel.

"Ah, young love," Larry said. Then putting his arms around my waist and drawing me close, he added, "Old love's not too bad, either."

Helen was attractive and witty and settled in as if she'd known us forever. When she and Daddy walked to the car, I nodded toward them and, borrowing from a Bogart line in *Casa Blanca*, quipped, "This could be the beginning of a beautiful friendship."

"Looking like it," Larry agreed.

My phone rang before daylight Monday morning. I yanked out my earplugs, turned down my sound machine, and answered. It was Metz.

"I know it's early," he began, "but I knew you'd want to hear this." The tone of excitement in his voice had me instantly awake. "I'm supposed to be on desk duty, but I told my captain that I was seeing this case through, come heck or high water, so he let me question Sarnecki again last night. It took some doing, but when I reminded him we had him for multiple murders and attempted murders, he eventually started singing like a canary."

189

"Multiple murders?" I whispered.

"Don't bother whispering," came a sleepy voice beside me. "Put it on speaker. I want to hear this, too."

"Yeah. I told him we knew he did away with Ray John and that we were days away from identifying the person who got torched in Jewel's – or rather, Carrie's – pickup. Add that to the attempted murder of two police officers and you, and I guaranteed him he'd be getting the death penalty unless we got some major cooperation."

"That must have gotten his attention," Larry said. "We've got you on speaker," he added by way of explanation.

"Indeed it did. It took some coaxing, but when he finally started talking, we couldn't shut him up. And best of all, he waived his right to an attorney. Said he didn't trust lawyers and they were all working for our side anyway."

"So what'd he tell you?" I urged.

"First, he confessed to breaking into Art's shop and clobbering him. He even admitted to killing Ray John, and then he clammed up. But when I told him we knew he couldn't have pulled off any more than that on his own, he decided to tell us exactly how smart he was."

"Which means?" I asked.

"He told us this wasn't his first 'rodeo' – that he'd done a lot more and a lot worse. And by acting like we were blowing that off as pure baloney, he got mad enough to start naming names and dates and crimes even from before all this."

"But what about Jewel?" I interrupted.

"I said we knew he'd burned her body in the pickup, and that's all it took for him to rave on about how stupid we cops were. He said Jewel was at the bottom of Five Mile Creek and – this is almost verbatim, 'one of those crazy ladies who stuck their noses in it had probably been swimming right over the top of her.'"

I shivered involuntarily at the thought of being in the water with Jewel Fitzhugh's body. "Oh, how awful," was all I could say.

"But what about the body in the truck?" Larry asked.

"Sarnecki said he didn't know the guy's name. Said he was some junkie he'd hired who tried to double-cross him. DNA results should be in within a week or two."

"That long?" I asked.

"We'll be darn lucky if it doesn't take longer than that. Labs everywhere are backed up. Only on TV do you get instant DNA results," Metz told us. "And I've got even more news. Sarnecki also I.D.'d the guy he'd been working for."

Larry and I were both sitting straight up and leaning over the phone at this point. "Who?" we chorused.

"He didn't know his real name. Just called him 'The Collector.' But his description led us to a British guy who's a collector of all sorts of high-end goods. Cyril Pennylegion," Metz said, "and he has a reputation …"

"… for taking advantage of other people," I finished his sentence. "There was something on the news about him a few nights ago."

"Apparently he's done a whole lot more than take advantage. According to our songbird, Pennylegion has been a busy little criminal since coming to the U.S."

"So did Sarnecki tell you where to find this creep?" I asked.

"Righto," Metz responded in a very unconvincing British accent. "We have the old chap in the nick as I speak."

"That's great news!" I exclaimed. "Congratulations! Sounds like you may wrap up a lot of open cases before this is over."

"We think so," Metz agreed. "Now we just have to hang onto him while we sort through this. Scotland Yard wants to have a chat with him, too."

"So is he talking?" I asked.

"You could say that," Metz answered. "Every time any of us open our mouths in his presence, he says the same thing: 'Solicitor.'"

My first call after hanging up with Metz was to Daddy and Millie. By now I was awake enough to think of making it a conference call so I could share the news with both of them at once. Daddy, of course, had heard from Metz before I did. To Millie, however, this was all news, and she was as elated as I to learn about Sarnecki's confession and the arrest of Cyril Pennylegion.

"I would've called you after I talked to Metz," Daddy said,

"but he said he wanted to give you the update himself. And now I'll let you two continue this conversation without me," he added, "and I'll talk to you later, ladies. I have a breakfast date with Helen at IHOP."

My next thought turned to Carrie. "I told Metz I'd go and break the news to Carrie about Jewel," I told Millie. "You want to go with me?"

"I would, but I have back-to-back appointments at the studio this morning. Please give her my love and let her know Bill and I will be remembering her and the grandkids in our prayers."

Carrie took the news calmly. I knew she'd do a better job of breaking it to Ray Ray, Sissy, and Nubbin with me out of the way, so I made a hasty retreat, promising to help with funeral arrangements and in any other way I was needed.

"I appreciate it, Judy. I truly do," Carrie said. "But until I see her body with my own eyes, I ain't givin' up hope." She nodded her head firmly. "No, sir. I ain't givin' up on my daughter."

En route home, I made a call to Mickey at WEEE. "I know you've already run a story about the arrest of Jimmy Sarnecki," I told him. "And you've probably already heard that the police have picked up Cyril Pennylegion, too," I continued. "But there's a lot you don't know, and I'm willing to pass that info to you under one important condition."

"Name it," Mickey said, his fingers already pounding a keyboard as we spoke.

"Under no circumstances are you to include my name or Millie's when you do the newscast. Deal?"

"Uh, deal," he promised. "But what do you and your cousin have to do with this?"

Thirty minutes and a lot of "Wow!" and "Unbelievable!" exclamations later, Mickey had exclusive details of the takedown, and I had his solemn oath to leave me and Millie out of the story.

32

Summer was winding down, and the search for Jewel's body had long been called off. Metz, Daddy, and a lot of other folks with experience in that type of recovery believed the body might never be found, since Five-Mile Creek flowed into Locust Fork, and Locust Fork flowed into the Black Warrior River, with each consecutive waterway being deeper, wider, and harder to search.

Jewel remained a subject neither we nor Carrie often brought up, but we all included her name in our prayers for Carrie and the children.

The lightning bugs were still out in full force as we sat on Carrie's newly constructed screened porch and enjoyed a feast of barbecued ribs, corn on the cob, baked beans, slaw, and garlic bread. Carrie had already warned us to save room for the banana pudding she had stashed in her fridge.

"Carrie Parker," Daddy proclaimed, "if I were a few years younger, I'd propose. Any woman as pretty as you who can cook like that would make any man a fine wife."

"Daddy!" I reminded him, "I don't think Helen would

appreciate you proposing to another woman. And besides, there are actually men who do the cooking these days."

"Well, I'm glad I'm not one of them," Larry declared.

"Me, too," chimed in Bill.

"Don't go gettin' too flatterin'," Carrie cautioned. "I can take credit for the rest of the meal, I reckon, but I ordered them ribs from Dreamland."

Once a single hole-in-the-wall in Tuscaloosa, Dreamland's ribs had become so famous, they'd opened more locations, including one on the Southside of Birmingham.

"I cut up the bananas for the puddin'," Ray Ray reminded his grandma. "And Sissy and Nubbin buttered the garlic bread."

"That you did," Carrie nodded, "reaching over to tousle her older grandson's hair.

Carrie and all three grandkids wore new outfits, plus Carrie sported her new hairstyle and a light application of flattering makeup. It was wonderful to look around and see the smiles on everyone's faces as we celebrated Carrie's newfound fortune.

Detective Metz had returned the Honus Wagner card to Carrie and surprised her with the news that he had already contacted some collectors who were eager to buy it. Wanting to avoid any publicity, Carrie had been grateful when Metz offered to meet with the collectors and hear their offers.

"Do you mind if I tell them?" Metz looked at Carrie and asked.

"Naw," she said, grinning. "If it weren't for all of y'all, I'd a never knowed it was worth anything."

"Our hostess here, Mrs. Carrie Parker," Metz said in his most formal tone, "received a cashier's check for $700,000."

Applause thundered around the table. "Carrie, that's fantastic!" I gushed. "We're all so happy for you."

"Yeah, it's gonna make things a might easier around here," she agreed. "I done got these young'uns enrolled in school here and they'll be startin' next week. They's all going to Glory Christian Academy. Ain't that somethin'?" she added.

"It's fabulous," Millie agreed. "Glory's a good school and they'll be taught the Bible along with their other lessons."

"They've done learned a lot since they been goin' to church with me," Carrie told us. "Matter of fact, Ray Ray's got somethin' he probably wants to tell hisself, don't you, baby?" She gazed at her grandson affectionately.

"I'm gettin' baptized next Sunday," he announced proudly.

"Well, the news just gets better and better!" Daddy said, reaching over and patting Ray Ray's shoulder.

"We wanna get baptisted, too," Sissy demanded, her bottom lip poked out in her very best pout.

"It's 'baptized,' Sissy," Ray Ray corrected his sister. "You can't just up and do it. First, you gotta give your heart to Jesus. That's what I did. You'll understand more when you're older. Like me," he added.

"Well, I ain't never gettin' baptized," declared the usually silent Nubbin, his mouth encircled with barbecue sauce.

"Why you wanna say a thing like that?" Sissy asked him.

"'Cause I can't swim and I don't like baths," he answered.

We all had a good laugh over that, but as soon as the children left the porch to catch lightning bugs, the conversation grew serious.

"You know," Carrie said quietly, "this money is a big blessin', but it's come at a high price. If Ray John or Jewel had told me that card was worth lots of money, I'd a shared with 'em. Now, as it is, I'm afraid they're both gone. But," she smiled, "I thank the good Lord ever' day for these young'uns and for trustin' me with such a big responsibility."

"It is that," I agreed.

"I'm tryin' to be a good steward," Carrie continued, "but I done spent a ton of money. I guess you seen when you come up that I got me a new truck. Well, not new, but new to me. Give $5,000 for it." She smiled. "And some of my church ladies has taught me how to drive it.

"Between it and this porch and the clothes and all, I've done been through nearly $9,000. Lord only knows what this porch would've cost if the church folks hadn't volunteered all the labor. Just talkin' about that kind of money sounds crazy."

"Not at all," I assured her. "This porch is a really nice addition to your home, and you needed transportation, so the truck wasn't frivolous, and the clothes sure weren't."

"I reckon you're right," she responded, "but it's an awful lot of money, and I'm used to pinchin' pennies. Which I still intend to do. It's just that, in the past, I ain't had much to pinch."

"We understand," Art assured her.

"And I done paid my tithe on that money, too," Carrie added. "I thought my preacher was gonna pass out when I give him that check." She grinned at the remembrance. "I'm gonna be careful, but I hope to do a lot of good for a lot of folks now that I'm able."

"That's great, Carrie," I told her, squeezing her hand.

"My bank set me up with a financial advisor," she went on. "Can you imagine me, Carrie Parker, havin' her own financial advisor?"

"You're doing the right thing," Detective Metz assured her. "That's a lot of money, but you've got three children's futures and your own to think of. Having a professional help you plan ahead is a smart move."

"I hope so," Carrie responded. "I intend to get a few repairs done around here and that oughta do it. But first I'm cleanin' this place out from top to bottom. I got junk stuck in ever' nook and cranny. I need to finish clearing out them two bedrooms for the kids. The closets and dressers is packed with stuff I ain't gone through since Methuselah was in diapers."

"Sounds like you're on your way to getting things organized," Larry commented.

"I'm workin' on it a bit at a time," she said. "And to think all of this started with a little ol' box of baseball cards."

The entire table went silent.

"You mean you have more baseball cards?" Bill questioned.

"Well, yeah," Carrie answered. "Don't y'all remember me

talkin' about my cigar box?" she asked, looking at the rest of us. "My grampaw collected them things and I got a whole boxful in the top of my closet."

"Mind if we take a look at them?" Metz asked.

Carrie's grandfather's baseball card collection turned out to be a substantial one. In addition to a number of players I've either never heard of or can't recall their names, she had cards for Albert Spalding, "Shoeless" Joe Jackson, and Babe Ruth. Metz was delighted when Carrie asked him to help with their sale.

Eight more cards brought in a tad over one million dollars. The rest of the cards, Carrie insisted on tucking away, this time in a safe deposit box. She says she plans to give one away to a different charity each year. And she has enough left to do that for the rest of her lifetime.

A Few Bargainomics Tips

Chapter 1: Ray John's recliner is probably beyond hope, but to hide worn fabric chair arms, shop around for a pair of machine washable fabric placemats of a color that coordinates with or is similar to your chair. Attach a couple of peel-and-stick Velcro® strips to the underside of the placemats and attach the corresponding strips to the chair arms. Presto, you've got no-sew arm covers that can be removed and washed as needed.

Chapter 2: In real life, I'm no longer doing my segments on WBRC Fox 6 TV, but I am speaking to churches and civic groups wherever I'm invited. I'm also posting a daily Bible study, bargains galore, travel tips, and other money-saving info on my website, www.Bargainomics.com, as well as on Facebook and Twitter. Search for *Bargainomics*.

Chapter 3: Speaking of my Fiery Sunset and Spicy Cedar hair, there's a big difference between using permanent and semi-permanent hair color, so always read the label to see which product you're considering. *Permanent* means the product literally changes the color of your hair, which also means as your hair grows, the new growth or "roots" will show the color difference and will need to be recolored regularly. *Semi-permanent* color simply puts a color or glaze over your natural color and will fade away after a dozen or so shampoos.

Chapter 6: How will I remove those pesky grass stains? Baking soda to the rescue! I'll make a paste of baking soda and water, then add a few drops of white vinegar. I'll dampen my khakis and cover the stains with my paste mixture, using a nail brush to scrub the stains out. A normal washing afterwards should have my pants as good as new.

Chapter 10: Newspaper makes excellent packing material to protect breakables during a move or when shipping or mailing, but it's also the best material you can use for cleaning your windows and mirrors. Spray the windows with "store-bought" window cleaner or make your own by filling a clean spray bottle with one cup isopropyl alcohol, one cup water, and one tablespoon white vinegar. Unlike cloth or paper towels, newspaper won't leave any lint or other residue. The only thing the black print will come off on is you, so it's a good idea to wear gloves.

Chapter 13: Even with the trailer door left open, Jewel could have kept a lot of those flying insects out by hanging homemade fly strips in the doorway. Here's a super easy way to make them: Cut a brown paper bag into inch-wide strips. In a saucepan, bring to a boil one cup of corn syrup and one cup of water. Remove the pan from the heat and drop in your paper strips. Allow these to soak for several hours. Carefully lift the strips from the saucepan and stretch them out on a cookie sheet to dry – the strips will still be very sticky. Use string or thumbtacks to hang several strips in every opening where there's a fly problem. Any insect that lands on the strip will find itself in an inescapably sticky situation.

Chapter 15: Whenever you're shopping, remember my motto: "Don't be afraid to ask; the worst thing they can tell you is, 'No.'" I didn't negotiate on the price of the yard sale toaster, but my $8 offer was accepted for the $10 jacket. While shopping for a lamp at a home improvement store, I found a whole section clearance-priced at 75 percent off. That meant the $100 lamps were now $25. After checking a number of boxes, I realized the display model was the only one remaining in the design I really wanted. Flagging down an employee, I showed him the lamp and asked, "Will you give me a bigger discount if I buy the display?"

I admit he did a bit of an eye roll, but he simply said, "I'll have to check with the manager." The stunned employee returned to me with an offer of a $20 reduction. I left the store with a $100 lamp for $5. Ask, and you just might receive.

Chapter 16: Unless you're super hungry, consider sharing a plate or splitting the entrée. Some restaurants add a small charge for this; even so, it can still mean a considerable savings.

Chapter 19: Whether you're using a charcoal or gas grill, don't fire it up to cook a measly few items. Fill the grill. When Larry and I grill, we load it with everything from chicken, beef, and pork to veggie skewers and more. We have one immediate meal and freeze the rest in meal-sized portions, so throwing together a grilled chicken salad or any other meal is a breeze.

Chapter 21: You aren't likely to run across a million-dollar baseball card while out junkin' through yard sales, thrift stores, and flea markets, but don't think it's beyond the realm of possibility. In 2014, a flea market shopper paid $25 for three paintings offered by one seller. These turned out to be the works of Jackson Pollock, a famous American abstract impressionist painter. Appraised value of the trio? More than 11 million dollars.

Chapter 22: Without my neighborhood watcher Clarice, I'd have had no idea that white Hyundai was anywhere around. A Neighborhood Watch program is a highly effective tool against crime. If you don't have one, consider starting one, even if you already have electronic surveillance around your home. You can find all the resources you'll need by going to the website of the National Crime Prevention Council, www.NCPC.org. Simply search for the phrase *neighborhood watch*.

What's Real?

Since I'm real, as well as several other characters and places in *A Bargain to Die For*, I thought I'd let you who and what else is real. If a person or place isn't listed below, they were plucked from my imagination, or weren't significant enough to the storyline to warrant further explanation. You'll also find some clarifications in the Acknowledgments. If you have questions about anyone or anyplace I didn't cover, email me at: *judywbates@bargainomics.com*.

- My husband Larry is real and he's every bit as handsome and sweet as I portray him. He's also a true Mr. Fix-It and an excellent mechanic. He really has a car collector friend named Terrell who, for many years, operated a garage where classic cars were restored to showroom appearance.

- Millie is my real live cousin, friend, shopping buddy, and Vanna White. She's also a multi-talented artist, even though, sadly, the old home place, her studio, and her pets come from my imagination. Her husband Bill is also real, and quite a hand at gardening.

- Chalybeate Springs was the original name for the city of Gardendale, Alabama.

- Smith Lake, or Lewis Smith Lake, is a beautiful manmade Alabama reservoir where Larry and I enjoy spending time whenever we can.

- I mention both real and fictitious thrift stores. To find real thrift and consignment shops wherever you live or travel within the U.S., go to *www.TheThriftShopper.com* and search for a specific city or zip code.

- The original Café Du Monde is located in the New Orleans French Market, but you can buy their delicious coffee and chicory online and at some grocers and specialty shops. There are several locations around the NOLA area now, including one at the airport. Make sure you try a beignet during your visit.

- Eric Johnson is a real up-and-coming artist. See his work and learn more at: *www.EricJohnsonArt.net*.

- Pretty much the whole world knows DQ (Dairy Queen) and Waffle House are real, but not everyone has experienced Milo's Hamburgers. I recommend the cheeseburger with grilled onions. And don't forget extra sauce for dipping your French fries. You'll find more info and a list of locations at: *www.MilosHamburgers.com.*

- The National Quartet Convention (where Larry and I really met our Norwegian friend Per and his brothers) is an annual gathering of Southern Gospel groups held in September, most recently at the LeConte Center in Pigeon Forge, Tennessee. To order tickets or learn more, visit: *www.NatQC.com.*

- Master Gardener Gwen was brought to life for this adventure, but in reality, my talented, beautiful, and funny friend lost her battle to ovarian cancer several years ago. Ladies, please have regular exams and don't ignore symptoms of this deadly disease. Read more at: *www.Ovarian.org.*

- Brookside is the actual hometown of my husband Larry, located right on the banks of Five-Mile Creek, where I added the fictitious Cheney's Mill.

- My and Larry's neighbor Clarice is real and one of the best cooks and friends a person could hope for.

- Bevill State Community College is located in Sumiton, Alabama, and includes a School of Cosmetology where well-supervised students can practice their skills on your hair and nails, and you can be pampered at a bargain price. Learn more at: *www.BSCC.edu.*

- Millie, Carrie, Rosa, and I did a little shopping at Macy's, particularly checking out the Last Act clothing. What's that? An entire section of super discounted clothing you'll find in every Macy's Department Store, as well as on their website. Find locations and shop online at *www.Macys.com.*

- Finally, the information about the illusive item The Collector was after is for real, but for those who may be reading this before finishing the book, you'll get no spoiler here!

More Bargainomics

Visit my website at www.Bargainomics.com and follow me on Facebook and Twitter.

Search for the word *Bargainomics*.

And watch for another Bargainomics Lady mystery coming soon!

BARGAINOMICS PUBLICATIONS

Made in the USA
Columbia, SC
15 November 2020

24602647R00120